DANGEROUS LIES

BADGE OF HONOR SERIES

LYNN SHANNON

DANGEROUS LIES

So do not fear, for I am with you; do not be dismayed, for I am your God. I will strengthen you and help you; I will uphold you with my righteous right hand.

Isaiah 41:10

ONE

"I'm being threatened."

Megan Ingles placed a series of printouts on the scarred table. Voices and the sound of phones ringing filtered through the closed door of the interview room. It was shift change at the Knoxville Police Department. The cluster of officers surrounding her should've been reassuring, but the block of ice lodged in her core refused to budge. Too many problems plagued her, and one of them sat directly across the table.

Detective Jax Taylor. His expression was frozen in a permanent scowl, heavy brows furrowed over a set of piercing blue eyes. The first button on his shirt was undone, providing a peek of tanned skin along his collarbone. A five-o'clock shadow darkened his jaw. Smudges under his lower lashes hinted he hadn't slept well lately. Megan imagined he'd been working night and day on his younger brother's case. Oliver died ten years ago, but as far as the Taylor family was concerned, the pain was still fresh. So was the anger.

They blamed her for Oliver's death.

Detective Noah Hodge pulled the printouts toward him and scanned the emails. Concern creased his features. Megan felt a flicker of relief. She didn't know Noah well, but she was friendly with his wife, Texas Ranger Felicity Capshaw. They were a lovely couple, and Megan had the impression Noah was a solid police officer. She prayed he would take the threats seriously.

"How long have you been receiving these?" Noah asked.

"For the last month. They've all been sent to my business email. Initially, I dismissed them as someone's idea of a sick joke, but lately..." A shiver ran down her spine. "The threats have grown more specific, and yesterday, it felt like someone was watching me leave work."

She'd read the emails repeatedly, enough to have them memorized. Key phrases stuck with her. *You can't escape what happened that night... You'll pay for what you've done... Justice will be served. I'll make sure of it.*

Her gaze drifted to Jax. His expression was stone cold. Unyielding and unconcerned. A spark of anger lit within her. "The emails started after it became public knowledge that you reopened the investigation into the accident. Someone is trying to scare me, and I'm worried they're seeking vigilante justice for Oliver's death."

She'd often had nightmares about that night. Oliver had been terrified when she picked him up on a lonely stretch of country road. High on drugs, his ramblings made little sense. Except for one thing: *He's going to kill us.*

Megan never found out who *he* was. A truck—or some other large vehicle—came up behind her compact sedan and rammed them. Terrified, Oliver had grabbed the wheel of Megan's car. While they struggled for control, the assailant rammed them again, sending their vehicle off the edge of an embankment.

Oliver was killed instantly. Megan, wounded and trapped in the wreck, sat all night next to her friend. Praying. Crying. Cold. Terrified that the attacker would return to finish the job. Now, with the investigation reopened, she feared not only that the killer might still be out there but that the renewed attention could expose her to further danger.

Goosebumps pebbled on her arms. Her gaze jumped between the two detectives. "Has there been any progress in finding the man who ran us off the road?"

Jax scoffed. "How could there be? We both know no one else was there." He pulled the printed emails closer and scanned them quickly before setting the pages aside. His steely gaze met hers. "I'm tired of these games, Ms. Ingles. When are you finally going to tell the truth about what happened that night?"

She closed her eyes, struggling for patience. "I have."

For a moment, Jax looked like he wanted to swear. Then he sucked in a breath and his expression shifted. He leaned forward, close enough for her to catch the scent of his aftershave. Something warm and spicy. His expression grew pleading. "My family has been through a lot. Losing Oliver... it's created a hole we can't fill. I know you cared about him too."

She had. They'd been friends. A toxic relationship—Megan understood that now—but back then, Oliver had been the only person who truly saw her. He recognized her trauma. She saw his. Together, they numbed those deep wounds with drugs. Oxy, mostly, but sometimes meth. A horrible coping mechanism that had nearly destroyed her.

After overdosing and almost dying, Megan went to rehab. She got clean, rediscovered her faith, and started therapy. She tried to talk Oliver into getting clean too, but he wasn't ready. So she cut ties with him as part of her sobriety program.

Megan shouldn't have gone to pick up Oliver that night. They hadn't spoken in months. But when he'd called, desperate and panicked, she'd gone anyway. Out of love for the friend she still cared about.

"Talking about what happened that night can be difficult." Jax kept his gaze locked on her. His eyes were a dark blue, the color of the ocean before a storm. "You didn't mean for it to happen. It was an accident. People make mistakes. I know that. Maybe you and Oliver had a lover's quarrel."

"No. We never dated." Megan had answered that question before too. "Our relationship was platonic."

"Okay, so you didn't fight, but mistakes still happen. If you were high that night—"

She slapped her hand down on the table. "I was not high." Megan's voice was too loud, her reaction too explosive, but her temper was fraying. The accusations weren't new. She'd been fighting against them since the first investigation of the accident ten years ago. "I was sober, had been for months. Someone *did* run us off the road. Oliver's killer is still out there. Why don't you care about that?"

"There's no physical evidence indicating anyone else was there," Noah replied. His expression was blank, but there was a hint of confusion buried in his tone. As if he wasn't sure who to believe. Megan or Jax. Both had theories about that night.

It frustrated Megan that no one believed her. In all fairness, she was partly to blame. Her rebellious teenage behavior had given her a reputation in Knoxville, and after the accident, she'd initially lied to investigators out of fear and worry for her own safety. But it'd been ten years. She was not the same eighteen-year-old. Now, Megan was a licensed therapist with a thriving practice in addition to running the local Narcotics Anonymous meetings. She attended church, donated her time to the library board, and took care of her elderly grandparents.

She'd worked hard to correct the mistakes of her past by being honest. A good member of the community. Most townsfolk had forgiven her, but there were some who still gave her the side-eye. Who believed she'd gotten away with murder.

People like Jax. Except he was a detective with the police department and had the power to uncover the truth. She needed him to listen with an open mind.

Megan blew out a breath and tried to steady her

emotions. "I was not high that night. Oliver called me, I went to pick him up, and when I did, he said someone was after him. Then we were run off the road." She leveled her gaze on Jax. "I want to help you, but I can't do that if you don't believe me."

He ignored her last statement. "You lied to investigators. You left town right after the accident."

"I was terrified Oliver's killer would come after me." Megan gestured to the emails. "Honestly, who's to say these emails aren't from him? They talk about vengeance, but that could mask the real purpose for wanting to hurt me. I'm the only witness to what happened that night. I don't think it's a coincidence that I started receiving threats shortly after the investigation into the accident was reopened."

Jax lifted a shoulder. "How do we know you didn't send these emails to yourself to garner sympathy?"

Her mouth dropped open. "You've got to be kidding."

Jax rose, palms planted on the table for leverage. He loomed over her. "No, I'm not kidding." The anger in his voice was sharp. "This innocent act may work on some people, but I'm not buying it. I know what happened. You were high or drunk, you picked up my brother for a joyride, and then you ran off the road. You didn't kill him on purpose, I'll give you that, but he's dead all the same. You're guilty of negligent homicide and terrified of going to prison, so you'll do whatever is necessary to muddy the waters of this investigation. Including sending yourself fake threats."

Megan trembled. "That's not true." Her words came

out weaker than she intended. Jax's accusations, while false, raked against her survivor's guilt. She blamed herself for Oliver's death. She'd failed to maintain control of the vehicle. "I'm sorry for everything your family has gone through, but I'm telling the truth about what happened that night. These threats are real…"

He didn't believe her. It was etched in every line on his handsome face. The contempt pouring from him was too much to take. She shrank back. Jax wouldn't physically harm her, but he'd love to slap some cuffs on her wrists and haul her to prison.

A headache pulsed at her temple. In desperation, she sought out Noah. She met his gaze. "Please look into the threats. Reexamine the evidence from the accident. Someone else *was* there. We were run off the road."

He gave a sharp nod, but his expression remained unreadable. Megan was normally intuitive. Reading people was a skill that came naturally, but right now, she had no idea what Noah was thinking. Would he follow up? Or would he ignore the threats the moment she stepped out of this room?

Either way, there was nothing more she could do. Her stomach swirled with a mixture of unease and frustration as she stood, gathering her purse and coat.

Jax rose to his full height. Broad shouldered and muscular, he had the physique of an athlete. A scar creased the edge of one furrowed brow. His shadowed jawline and dark mop of hair gave him a hardened appearance—the look of a man who had spent too much time in the trenches of life. Megan knew only a little about him personally. He'd worked undercover with the ATF for nearly ten years before joining the Knoxville Police Department. People described him as serious, dedicated, and uncompromisingly honest.

In another life, maybe they could've been friends, but Oliver's addiction and his death had set them on a different path. To Jax, she was the enemy, the person to blame. And while Megan didn't carry that same bitterness, trusting him would be foolish. After this meeting, she wasn't sure she could rely on anyone in the police department.

It was a crushing and lonely feeling. One that reminded her far too much of her teenage years.

Jax's piercing blue eyes followed Megan as she went to the door. As she reached for the knob, he said, "This isn't over. I won't stop until I get to the truth."

Megan glanced over her shoulder, meeting his intense gaze. This time when she spoke, her voice was steady. "I pray that's true."

Their eyes held for a beat. A flicker of something—regret, confusion, or perhaps another feeling entirely—flashed across Jax's face, but in the next moment, it was gone, hidden behind the same hardened mask she was familiar with.

Noah sat quietly. His rejection stung. She'd thought they were friends. Or at least acquaintances. At the very least, she'd hoped Noah would honor his oath to protect *all* citizens of the town. Megan ignored the wave of disappointment that struck her as she swung open the door to the interview room.

No one believed her. She was alone. Being stalked by God knows who.

It was terrifying.

Tears pressed against her eyelids. She wouldn't cry. Not in front of all these people. Head held high, she crossed the main room of the police department and exited the building. A slap of cold air stole her breath. Megan quickly shrugged on her coat as she hurried across the dark parking lot toward the street. Her office was a short distance from the police department. It didn't make sense to drive in the daylight, but the meeting had taken longer than expected. Now, with the cold January darkness pressing in, Megan regretted not taking her car.

Her heels tapped against the pavement. At this hour, traffic was nonexistent. The street lights flashed yellow. Megan jaywalked at an angle to the main square. Tree leaves whispered in the wind, the creepy sound heightening her anxiety. She huddled inside her coat and quickened her steps.

Clearview Counseling, her workplace, came into view. The converted shotgun house had a quaint charm, with white shutters and a small front porch. Megan worked there along with another two therapists and several members of support staff. The adjacent parking lot was empty save for her SUV tucked under the bright beam of a streetlight.

Megan fumbled with the fob to unlock the doors. The headlights on her vehicle flashed. She rushed into the driver's seat, shivers racing through her body from the icy weather. She started the SUV and exited the parking lot. The pounding at her temple increased. A migraine was coming on. A stress headache. Megan might stave it off with a hot bath and a home-cooked meal.

Megan stopped at a red light at the edge of town. Nana and Pops would be waiting for her. The thought of her loving grandparents eased some of the tension in Megan's muscles. Returning to Knoxville hadn't been easy, but even with these recent threats, she didn't regret it. Nana and Pops were advancing in years, and Nana's recent bout with cancer had been a stark reminder of how precious their time together was. Megan intended to make the most of it. Her grandparents were all the family she had left.

The town faded as she followed the curve of Main Street. The engine hummed, and now that it'd warmed up, Megan reached for the knob to turn on the heater.

A shape loomed in her rearview mirror.

Megan screamed and nearly drove off the road as an arm encircled her shoulders like a vise, pushing her back against the seat. A round circle touched her throat, pressing hard. Her muscles locked in terror.

"Nice and steady," a voice whispered against her earlobe. "I won't hurt you as long as you do as I say. Got it?"

The man was crouched behind her, his face covered by a ski mask. Dim light coming from the dash of her vehicle illuminated the cold steel of the handgun pressed to Megan's throat. She gripped the steering wheel until her knuckles went white. Terror clogged her throat. She wasn't stupid enough to believe this man wouldn't harm her.

The threats had been real.

And now, he was going to do as he promised in the emails.

He was going to kill her.

TWO

Things were becoming complicated.

Jax twirled a pen between his fingers and studied the emails Megan had left behind. The initial messages were vague, but as time went on, the threats became more specific, as if the sender was spiraling into an obsession.

"I have to take these emails seriously," Noah said, perching on the edge of Jax's desk with his long legs stretched out in front of him.

"I know." Jax leaned back in his chair. "I'm not saying you shouldn't investigate, but keep an open mind. These messages could have come from anyone—a random guy holed up in his mom's basement, bored and looking to scare someone, for example. And frankly, I wouldn't put it past Megan to fake them. She's a liar."

Noah was quiet for a moment before he replied, "I find her explanation compelling. Assuming Megan's version of events is true—"

"Which version?" Jax interrupted, his tone laced with sarcasm. "The first or the second?"

Noah shot him a warning look. "The second. At the time of the accident, she was a terrified young woman who'd just been run off the road by an unknown assailant. Megan had a criminal history. She'd been arrested a few times for drug possession and those cases were pending. Her relationship with the police wasn't a good one. I can see why she'd omit certain facts the first time she was questioned."

"It's just as likely she lied to protect herself," Jax countered. "Megan initially told investigators she lost control of the vehicle. Once word got out about the accident, people started blaming her for Oliver's death. Townsfolk figured Megan was high. Two days later, she fabricates this story about someone chasing them to avoid taking the blame."

Jax considered this to be the most likely scenario. Addicts were notorious liars. Oliver had been using for nearly a year before their parents discovered the truth. He'd lied, manipulated, and dodged consequences over and over again. Megan had also been skilled at wriggling out of trouble. She'd been arrested on drug charges and shoplifting, but only received a slap on the wrist.

It'd been ten years since the accident, and from everything Jax had learned about Megan, she'd turned her life completely around. She worked as a therapist, ran the local Narcotics Anonymous meetings, took care of her elderly grandparents and regularly attended church. Deep down, he admired the changes she'd made. But getting sober and helping others didn't erase the past. Some mistakes had lifelong repercussions.

"You said it yourself," Jax continued. "There's no physical evidence anyone was on the road with them that night. No skid marks other than Megan's. No broken tail-light fragments on the road or scrapes of paint on her bumper. Her story doesn't check out."

Noah frowned. "Her vehicle was damaged after going over the embankment. The crime scene photos are terrible, and there aren't any pictures of her car after it was towed. I can't say with certainty she wasn't run off the road. As for the assumption she was high at the time of the crash... there's no evidence of that either. She tested negative for drugs and alcohol at the hospital."

"Those tests were done over twelve hours after the accident," Jax pointed out. Megan's car was found by a farmer heading to his fields the morning after the crash. "Depending on what she'd taken, it may not have shown up on a tox screen."

"Come on, Jax. You know as well as I do that oxy and meth stay in the system for days. Oliver tested positive for both. If they'd been using together, like they'd done in the past, it would have shown up in her bloodwork."

Noah was right, but Megan's behavior didn't fit the mold of someone who was innocent. "She left town a week after the accident. Packed up and ran."

"A reasonable response if she feared retribution from the person who'd run her off the road."

Frustration and anger simmered in Jax. His jaw tightened. "Seems to me you've already made up your mind about the investigation. You don't believe she's responsible, do you?"

He sighed. "The investigation was flawed from the beginning. There are missing reports, and the crime scene photographs are shoddy. The only witness statements are Megan's. I've gone over everything more than once, but the result is the same. Based on the evidence we have, Megan hasn't broken any laws. I know that's not what you want to hear, but it's the truth."

Jax knew Noah was right. Mentally, he understood. But emotionally, he wasn't ready to let it go. "I don't believe there's nothing else we can do. How about interviewing my brother's friends again?" He crossed his arms over his chest. "Or are you ready to end the investigation because of your friendship with Megan?"

Noah stiffened. "Careful, Jax. I understand how important this is to you, and I sympathize with what you've been through, but that accusation is insulting. I'd never look the other way if there was proof a crime had been committed."

Jax took a deep breath, exhaling slowly. "You're right. I'm sorry. That was over the line."

Wariness settled over him like a wet blanket. The police department was short on staff. He'd been working double shifts for days and then combing over his brother's case in his free time. The stress and lack of sleep were making him short-tempered and unreasonable. Jax scraped a hand over his jaw. "I know this case puts you in a difficult position."

"I follow the evidence wherever it leads. Nothing

difficult about that." Noah was quiet for a moment. "But I would like to make a personal observation. Something for you to think about. Drug users do lie, and most people have secrets, but in our line of work, it's easy to become jaded and suspicious of everyone. Megan made mistakes in her youth, there's no doubt about that, but the woman I've come to know is caring, empathetic, and responsible. I genuinely believe that if she'd caused Oliver's death, she'd say so and accept the consequences of her actions."

"Even if it meant prison time?" Jax couldn't keep the note of disbelief out of his voice.

Noah met his gaze. "Even if it meant prison time."

There wasn't a hint of hesitation in Noah's response. Jax had worked with him long enough to form a deep respect for his skills and ability. Noah wasn't a fool, nor was he sloppy. If he believed Megan would take accountability for her mistakes, then Jax needed to at least consider his perspective.

"Why do you think that?" he asked.

"From the beginning of this investigation, she's answered every one of my questions. She's been forthright and consistent. Read the reports again. Yes, she wasn't truthful in her initial explanation of the accident, but once she came forward to revise her statement, it remained the same. Honestly, Jax, I believe someone ran her and Oliver off the road that night. I think we need to reevaluate the case from the beginning and look at alternative suspects, starting with anyone who may have wanted your brother dead."

This was opening a whole new avenue of investigation, one Jax wasn't certain would lead anywhere, but it was worth thinking about. "Let's talk about this more tomorrow. It's been a long day."

"Sure." Noah clapped a hand on his shoulder. "I've got your back. Never doubt that."

Jax nodded, but his heart felt heavy and worries crowded his mind. What if they never found the truth? Oliver's death haunted him. It'd been easy to push back the grief when he was working undercover for the ATF in Atlanta, but moving back home last year had brought those buried feelings to the surface. Seeing the way Oliver's death had affected his entire family made things worse.

Jax wanted to fix it. He wanted closure. Justice. The thought that he might not get it... well, that was a bitter pill to swallow.

He packed up his desk and headed for his truck. The cool night air felt good on his flushed skin, but it did little to clear his head. Megan's parting words echoed in his mind. *I pray you do.* If she truly was responsible for Oliver's death, would she really want him to find the truth? Or was this just another way to manipulate the case? Jax wanted to believe it was the latter, but something in her voice... he could've sworn in that moment, Megan was telling the truth. And she had seemed genuinely terrified by the emails.

Jax had accused Noah of letting his feelings impede the investigation, but maybe... maybe he was the one not seeing things clearly.

A dark shape on the side of the road caught his attention, pulling him abruptly from his thoughts. As he drew closer, his headlights flashed across a Toyota RAV4, parked half on, half off the narrow country road. The driver's side door hung open. No one was inside the vehicle, at least from what he could see.

Weird. An uneasy prickle ran down his spine. Jax flipped on his turret lights and radioed Angie, their night dispatcher. "Can you run a plate number for me?" he asked, rattling off the letters and numbers as he scanned the tree line bordering both sides of the road. The lake glimmered faintly in the distance.

Angie's voice crackled over the radio. "Got a name for you, Detective. Owner of the vehicle is Megan Ingles."

Concern sank deep claws into him. "I'm going to investigate further. Stand by."

"10-4."

Jax grabbed his flashlight and portable radio before exiting the truck. His training took over, his mind cataloging every detail. No visible damage on the rear bumper. Tires intact. The Toyota was still running, headlights on, but the overhead light inside was off. Loose gravel crunched under his boots and his breath fogged in the cold air as Jax drew closer to the open driver's side door. His flashlight picked up a dark stain on the panel.

Blood.

More speckled the steering wheel and the dash. He tightened his grip on the flashlight, angling it across the interior. "Megan?"

No response. Her purse lay on the floor, cell phone in the cup holder. No jacket. More blood peppered the floorboards and seat. Jax's heart rate kicked into over-drive. He pressed the button on his portable radio. "Angie, I need a patrol car at my location."

What on earth had happened here? The blood was concerning, but it wasn't enough to indicate a violent assault. She could've hurt herself somehow. And then... what? Disappeared, leaving her car running and her door open? No. It seemed more likely she'd escaped from the vehicle. This area of the lake was a protected nature reserve. No houses, no stores. It was deserted at this hour.

Something was wrong. Very wrong.

He scanned the area around the vehicle, searching for any sign of Megan. His mind clung stubbornly to the idea that she might have staged this, just like the emails. It was a horrible thought, but Jax didn't want to believe someone had truly been after her. Because if they were, he might already be too late.

He swept the flashlight toward the lake, glimpsing a path through the tall grass. The flattened stalks suggested someone had run across in a hurry. Jax followed the trail.

A scream tore through the night.

THREE

A hand clamped down on her ankle, dragging Megan from her makeshift hiding spot. Stones and jagged bark clawed at her back, tearing her skin. She screamed. The sound was instinctive. Primal. Animalistic. Her chest tightened with terror as the attacker yanked her toward him. His grip was bruising. Blood matted her hair and dripped down her neck from the pistol-whipping she'd received while escaping her vehicle. He'd already fired at her once—and missed—as she fled into the woods. But Megan knew at such close range, she didn't stand a chance.

This was a fight for her life.

Desperate, she kicked out with her other foot. The pointed heel of her boot landed somewhere in his midsection. He cursed, but his grip on her ankle didn't loosen, and he kept yanking her toward him. She threw a rock, but it bounced off his shoulder, useless. His other hand lifted, the gun clasped tightly in his fingers.

She twisted hard before he could take aim, throwing her weight to the side just as he squeezed the trigger. The bullet struck the dirt behind her. Her sudden movement threw the assailant off balance, and his grip on her ankle slipped. Taking her chance, Megan scrambled backward. Her fingers stumbled over a thick tree branch. She snatched it up and stood, swinging it like a club at the attacker's head.

Vibrations coursed up her arm as the tree branch hit home. The attacker cried out and his knees buckled.

Megan dropped the branch and ran.

Blindly, she tore through the thick woods. Branches snagged at her clothes and her boots—made for casual walks and professional outings—slipped on the pine needles. Her heart pounded. It was hard to breathe. Megan's exercise of choice was yoga. She wasn't prepared for a panicked run through the woods with a killer on her heels. Survival depended on getting to her car. Hopefully, the keys were still inside, and she'd be able to escape. If not...

She'd die.

The problem was, her assailant would expect her to head for the road. Would he beat her there? He'd proven adept at flushing her out, finding her hiding place within seconds. It probably didn't help that Megan was crashing through the woods like a runaway herd of horses. Terror narrowed her vision and her chest squeezed tight. Her foot caught on a tree root, and she stumbled, barely catching herself. Pain radiated from her shoulder and head as she collided with a tree.

Megan whimpered as the wound in her scalp blazed with fiery agony. Her vision blurred. Blood flowed from the gash, coating her skin and soaking into her sweater. Her legs shook with fear and exhaustion. She sucked in a deep breath, trying to loosen the vise around her midsection and relieve the cramp at her side. The road, and her vehicle, were nearby. Weren't they? She'd gotten turned around in her frantic desire to escape. Megan scanned the thick brush. There... up ahead. She had to keep moving.

A branch broke behind her.

Dear heaven, he was close.

A fresh dose of terror shot through Megan. She shoved away from the tree and bolted for the road. Her heart thundered in her chest. Tree limbs slapped her face and more roots threatened to trip her. She glanced over her shoulder, half expecting a bullet to pierce her. Though she couldn't see him, she sensed him in the dark. Megan willed her legs to keep moving.

A looming shape appeared ahead of her. She cried out in horror and attempted to slide to a stop, but a set of arms grabbed her. Every muscle in her body went rigid. Megan couldn't use her hands to protect herself—they were trapped next to her body—so she thrashed in a wild attempt to save herself.

"Stop." The command was harsh and authoritative. "It's Jax, Megan. Stop."

The words sliced through her panic. Tossing her hair out of her face, she glanced up. Moonlight filtered through the trees and highlighted half of Jax's face. It painted the curve of his left cheek and the fine line of his brow in an ethereal light. The other half was cast in shadow. His focus was locked on the woods behind her.

Relief, sharp and nearly overwhelming, weakened her limbs. Jax pulled her into the shadows. Only when he released her did she notice the gun in his hand.

"Who's chasing you?" The words were whispered but urgent. His focus never left the woods.

"I don't know." Her breath was shallow, her heart still racing. Despite the frigid weather, sweat coated her hairline. She shivered. "He has a gun."

Jax went still, holding a finger to his lips to silence her. Megan tensed, her gaze following his to the woods. Nothing moved, but she sensed a presence nearby. The hair on the back of her neck stood on end. Trembles began coursing through her body, and she hugged herself to keep from shaking.

Jax gently pushed her farther into the shadows until Megan's back bumped into a giant pine tree, and then he took a position in front of her. Shielding her. Feet planted, he stood close enough for her to feel his body heat. His broad shoulders blocked her vision and the scent of his cologne enveloped her like a blanket.

An indescribable feeling of safety washed over her. There was a killer nearby, but Megan had no doubts Jax would defend her. With his life, if necessary. It was a humbling and confusing realization. He hated her. And right now, he was protecting her.

A twig snapped. Jax's head swiveled, but he didn't shift an inch away from her. Megan placed her hands on his back. The move was instinctive. Her head throbbed, and with her vision swimming, she feared she might collapse. Unlike her tense form, his muscles were loose and fluid. He reached back and placed a reassuring hand on her arm. That small gesture of comfort, amid this terrifying experience, nearly broke her. She bit her lip to keep the tears at bay.

Leaves rustled. Closer this time. Megan could feel the killer's presence. Did he know Jax was protecting her? Could he see them? Or was he searching the woods for her? It would be harder to find Megan now that she'd stopped moving, although he'd successfully uncovered her previous hiding spot.

If he found them, he'd shoot them both.

Please, God, help us. We need you.

FOUR

Moonlight filtered through the trees overhead, casting deep shadows across the woods. Jax couldn't see the assailant, but he could sense him. The man was close. It was tempting to call out—to order him to surrender—but doing so could put them in even greater danger. Megan had said the attacker had a gun. Jax wouldn't risk drawing attention to their hiding spot, not with a civilian in the line of fire. His priority had to be her safety.

He adjusted his grip on his gun while keeping a protective stance in front of Megan. Her breaths were shallow, her muscles trembling as she clutched the back of his jacket, but she remained mercifully quiet and still. Life-and-death situations elicited an array of reactions in people—from sheer panic to complete immobilization and everything in between. Megan was terrified but hadn't lost her head. Jax was grateful for that. This situation would have been infinitely worse if she'd frozen in fear or succumbed to hysteria.

Nearby, leaves rustled. Jax's pulse jumped as he shifted his stance, scanning the shadows for the attacker. There—a darker shape, almost indiscernible against the thick brush. Could he see them? Jax wasn't sure. His muscles tensed as he raised his weapon. Behind him, Megan's breath hitched, and her body went utterly still.

The distant wail of sirens pierced the silence, faint at first but growing louder. A momentary blip of relief coursed through Jax. Finally. Backup was coming. He didn't lower his weapon or shift from his protective stance. The next few seconds were critical. Desperation could make the attacker reckless, causing him to shoot wildly in an attempt to eliminate witnesses.

Time slowed as the seconds ticked by. Jax could feel the other man weighing his choices. Then, as if spurred by the approaching sirens, the assailant bolted. Jax glimpsed a shadowy figure darting through the trees, the crunch of underbrush trailing behind him as he headed for the lake. Moments later, the sound of a motor filled the air. Not a car or a motorcycle. A boat.

Jax let out the breath he'd been holding and lowered his weapon. He turned to face Megan. She was completely hidden in the shadows, her shape barely distinguishable from the large pine tree he'd used to protect her flank. "Are you hurt? Can you walk?"

"I'm okay." Her voice trembled slightly. "I want out of these woods."

He gently took her elbow, and together, they headed for the road. As they broke away from the tree line, two patrol cars arrived. Jax lifted his hand in a wave as Tucker

Colburn exited from the first vehicle, his weapon already drawn. Former military, he'd joined the police force around the same time as Jax. The two men had formed a friendship over the last year.

"One perpetrator," Jax said, in lieu of a greeting. "Escaped on a boat. There's an old ramp about a mile through those trees. Make sure you secure the area all the way from the road to the lake."

Tucker nodded, his sharp gaze shifting to Megan. "Paramedics are on the way."

Jax glanced at Megan, and his breath hitched. Blood coated the side of her face, matting her silky blonde hair. In the strobing red and blue lights, her complexion looked waxy. Her torn jacket hung awkwardly on her shoulders, twigs and mud clinging to her clothes. Jax was still holding on to her elbow and felt her tremble, but she tried to offer Tucker a weak smile.

"I'll be fine." Her teeth chattered slightly. "Just need to sit down for a minute."

She was anything but fine. Megan was crashing from the adrenaline surge that could easily spiral into shock. Fresh concern coursed through Jax, tangled with a sharp wave of guilt. She'd been threatened, and Jax hadn't believed her. He'd outright accused her of lying.

"I've got Megan." Jax steered her toward his SUV. "Secure the scene, Tucker. And call Noah. He's the lead investigator."

Tucker nodded, reaching for the radio secured on his shoulder as he headed toward the other officer at the tree line. Jax hurried across the grassy median with Megan, the SUV's headlights blinking as they approached. The vehicle unlocked automatically, thanks to the fob in his pocket. Megan stumbled, nearly collapsing onto the asphalt, but Jax's firm grip kept her upright.

Jax opened the rear hatch and guided her toward it. "Sit."

She did as he instructed, hugging herself in a poor attempt to ward off the shakes. Jax quickly located his first-aid kit. "What happened?"

"He hid in my vehicle behind the seat. I didn't see him until he held a gun to my throat."

Jax wrapped an insulated blanket around her shoulders. Megan wasn't petite, but her willowy frame and delicate features gave her a vulnerable appearance. Freckles dusted her upturned nose. The mascara coating her long lashes had smeared under her eyes, and the haunted look in those mahogany-colored orbs hit him with another wave of guilt.

He cracked a heat pack, activating the chemicals, and pressed it into her hands. "Did you recognize him?"

She shook her head. "He wore a ski mask. Told me that if I did what he said, he wouldn't hurt me. I didn't believe him, so when he ordered me to turn onto a smaller dirt road, I slowed down to escape the vehicle." Her hand drifted to the matted blood in her hair. "He hit me with the gun while I was undoing my seat belt."

Anger heated Jax's blood. A man kidnapping a woman at gunpoint and pistol-whipping her was abhorrent. No matter his personal feelings about Megan, she didn't deserve this.

Jax gently lowered her hand from her wound and pressed a cold pack against the swollen goose egg. "Did he tell you where he was taking you?"

"No." Megan winced as the pack made contact.

"Sorry." He adjusted it, his tone soft. This close, he caught a faint whiff of her perfume, something light with a hint of vanilla. It felt strange to be this close to her. Jax didn't hate her—not exactly. Years in law enforcement had taught him that sometimes good people make terrible choices, especially when drugs and alcohol are involved. Megan wasn't evil, but he blamed her for Oliver's death and the pain it brought his family.

The investigation—his push to prove her guilty of negligent homicide—might have put her in the crosshairs. Knoxville was a small town, and the Taylors were well-liked. Had someone loyal to his family decided to take justice into their own hands? Based on the threats Megan had received, it seemed likely. Jax wasn't responsible for her attack tonight—the man who assaulted her was—but it didn't ease his conscience one bit.

Shoving those thoughts aside, he focused on tonight's attack. "Did you recognize his voice?"

Her brows furrowed as she considered the question. "If I did, it didn't register. I was scared and focused on surviving. He shot at me as I ran into the woods but missed. I tried to outrun him, but that didn't work, so I hid." Her lips quivered as she pressed them together. "He found me. We fought, and then I ran into you while trying to get back to my car."

Their gazes met, and the gratitude in Megan's eyes

did funny things to him. Jax didn't want to dwell on the implications of saving her life. It was his job. He'd do it again without hesitation, but everything that'd transpired tonight had created a mass of confusing feelings he didn't know how to untangle. Nor did he want to.

It was easier to be angry with her.

Jax asked Megan a few more follow-up questions, but none of her answers provided a clue as to the attacker's identity. Fifteen minutes later, she was sitting in the back of an ambulance, being tended to by paramedics.

Noah had arrived on the scene, and as Jax crossed the road to join him, their boss, Chief Sam Garcia, pulled up in his unmarked SUV. The chief's uniform was freshly ironed, but whiskers shadowed his usually clean-shaven jaw, and exhaustion weighed heavily on his posture. Jax knew his boss had left work on time that evening—an uncommon occurrence for a man known to work ten- or twelve-hour days. Jax imagined the chief was frustrated about being pulled into the cold night, but not a hint of that complaint was anywhere in his expression as he approached.

Chief Garcia greeted both detectives with a curt nod. "Report."

Jax walked him through everything they knew so far, starting with the threatening emails Megan had received and ending with the assailant's escape. "I think he had a boat tied to the old ramp and used it to get away."

Noah let out a low whistle. "If that's the case, this was an extremely well-planned attack. Knoxville is only five miles away, an easy distance to walk or run. So the assailant brings a boat here, ties it to the old ramp, runs to town, breaks into Megan's car, lies in wait, then holds her at gunpoint and forces her to drive here."

"But did he plan to take her on the boat?" Garcia asked. "Or did he plan to kill her?"

None of them could answer with certainty, but Jax had a theory. "He shot at her when she was escaping. I think the plan was always to kill her. It would've been easy to murder her, then use the boat ramp to drive her Toyota into the lake. Then he uses his boat to get back home or to his car."

Noah nodded. "This route isn't anywhere near Megan's house. No one would think to look for her here, and by hiding her car, it would've appeared as if she left town on her own."

The thought of how close the killer had come to succeeding made Jax's stomach churn. His gaze shifted to the back of the ambulance. Through the open doors, Megan sat on a stretcher with blankets piled over her lap and an ice pack pressed against her head.

"Whoever is behind this won't stop." Years of working undercover had taught Jax plenty about criminals. Most acted out of desperation or self-preservation, but there were always a few who identified with a mission. Those were the most dangerous. "He failed this time, but I think he'll try again."

"I'm afraid I agree with you." Garcia rocked back on his heels, his expression grim. "I want to see these emails as soon as possible. We'll need to comb the entire crime scene for evidence. Megan's vehicle will be towed to the state evidence shed for processing—fingerprints, DNA, anything we can find. If we're lucky, the guy wasn't wearing gloves when he broke into her car."

"He wore a ski mask," Noah added, his tone thoughtful, "which suggests the attacker is someone Megan knows. If this is connected to the threatening emails—and I don't see why it wouldn't be—then the perpetrator is probably local."

"Agreed." Garcia's sharp, steely gaze landed on Jax. "Detective, may I speak with you privately for a moment?"

Jax nodded and followed his boss a few steps away. The chief's expression was a hard mask of professionalism, but there was a hint of regret buried in his dark eyes. "I'm sorry to ask this, but it has to be done. Could your brother Wesley be responsible for this?"

Jax stiffened. "No, sir." The words were spoken automatically and emphatically. "No one in my family would do this. Including Wesley."

"Your brother has the brains and the knowledge to pull something like this off. He has a temper and has been in trouble with the law before—"

"Years ago. As a teenager." A bad temper was an inherited trait among the Taylor men, Jax included. These questions were striking against that temper, like flint against steel, but he was smart enough to keep his tone even. "Wesley hasn't stepped out of line since leaving the military. He barely leaves his cabin these days."

Jax's younger brother—Oliver's fraternal twin—had

once been adventurous and daring. Quick to laugh, impossibly intelligent, and popular were words everyone used to describe him. Now Wesley was a shell of his former self. A stint in the military that'd included numerous deployments and months as a prisoner of war had scarred him in every way. Physically, mentally, and emotionally. He lived off the grid in a log cabin he'd built by hand on a swatch of land that'd once belonged to their grandparents.

Chief Garcia lifted his cowboy hat and ran a hand through his salt-and-pepper hair. "Can you think of anyone else who might be capable of this?"

"No, sir."

The assault had been too meticulously planned for the average criminal. As much as Jax loathed to admit it, the chief had a point. Wesley was smart enough, and had the skills, to pull an attack like this off. Grief could twist and morph into anger and hatred, but murder? Jax wouldn't believe his brother was capable of it.

Arguing that point wouldn't get him far with the chief, but logic could. "If Wesley was behind this, Megan would be dead. He wouldn't have given her an opening to escape, and he wouldn't have missed the shot when she ran into the woods. He's an expert sharp-shooter."

The chief was quiet for a long moment and sighed. "Based on your brother's military record, you may be right. I still have to question him though."

Jax felt a surge of protectiveness, but battled it back and gave a sharp nod. Chief Garcia was only doing his job. Once Wesley was eliminated as a suspect, the investigation would turn toward finding the real perpetrator.

Chief Garcia settled his hat back on his head. "I'll interview Megan. Then I want you to go with her to the hospital. Until we know what we're dealing with, I want her protected. Don't leave her side for any reason."

Jax stiffened. Saving Megan's life tonight had been about duty. Taking on the role as her bodyguard, however, felt like a betrayal to his brother's memory. "Sir, I'd prefer that assignment go to someone else. And I'm sure Megan would too, given the history between us."

"I understand your feelings, Detective, and Megan's, but based on what we know so far, someone thinks killing her will get justice for Oliver." Chief Garcia gave him a knowing look. "By protecting Megan, you're sending the message that this isn't what your family wants."

Jax's back teeth clenched. He wanted to argue, to insist someone else take the assignment, but once again, the chief had a good point. He exhaled sharply, forcing himself to nod. "Understood, sir."

Chief Garcia nodded and then marched toward Megan in the ambulance. She was still pale, but someone —probably the paramedic—had wiped the blood and dirt off her face. Jax's stomach churned. The doubts Noah planted earlier tonight were sprouting roots and growing. Megan had been telling the truth about the threatening emails. Which begged the question: what else was she being honest about? Had Jax made a terrible mistake in assuming she was lying about the accident?

And in doing so, had he put her in danger?

FIVE

Megan opened her eyes, and panic gripped her chest. The ceiling above her was unfamiliar, the bedsheets felt rough and scratchy against her skin. Her heart rate spiked, and the pounding in her head intensified. Nausea churned as the remnants of a nightmare—running through the woods, chased by a masked killer—collided with the disorienting reality of her surroundings.

"You're okay." Movement on her left preceded a firm hand taking hers. The touch was unfamiliar. She turned her head to find Jax sitting in a chair next to her bed. His chin and cheeks were covered in thick whiskers, his dark hair a tousled mess as though he'd been running his hands through it. Faint morning light filtered through the window behind him.

Jax's brows creased with concern. "Are you in pain? I can call a nurse."

She shook her head to stop him, wincing at the sharp throb that followed the movement. The pain was manageable, a dull ache compared to the vivid terror of the nightmare that'd left her heart racing. Her surroundings sharpened into focus. A hospital room. She remembered being admitted last night for observation after being diagnosed with a concussion. It'd taken ten stitches in her scalp to close the wound from the pistol-whipping. Tests, bloodwork, an MRI, and a litany of paperwork had left her drained. She must've fallen asleep.

Jax released her hand and poured water into a cup. He held it to her lips, and the cool liquid soothed her parched throat. She felt as weak as a newborn, her hands trembling as she reached to take the cup from him. Megan drank again, the second sip easing her headache slightly more.

He frowned. "You look pale, like you're hurting. The doctor said you could have pain medication. I'll call a nurse—"

"No." She stopped him with a hand on his arm. His shirtsleeve was soft beneath her fingertips. "As a former addict, I avoid taking prescription pain medication if I can help it." Megan hadn't used drugs in over ten years, but she was hyper-aware of how fragile that recovery could be. She drew in a breath and some of her nausea faded. "I'll be okay. How long have I been asleep?"

"Only a few hours." Jax reclaimed the chair next to her bed. He was still wearing the same clothes from last night. The man hadn't left her side since climbing into the ambulance, except for the brief time she was changing into a hospital gown.

Jax's protection was both awkward and comforting.

Guilt, heartbreak, and anger were intrinsic to all their interactions, and yet, Megan knew he would never let anyone to harm her. He'd proven that last night when he saved her life. The gratitude she felt added a layer to their already complicated relationship. Megan wasn't sure how to navigate the tangled mess.

"Is it common to avoid pain medication?" Jax asked, cutting through Megan's thoughts. "For addicts, I mean."

"Everyone is different, but as a general rule, it's a good idea to avoid any addictive substances. Oxy was my drug of choice, so I'm especially careful with any kind of pain medication. I also have regular check-ins with my sponsor. Prayer helps too. Recovery isn't a one-and-done thing. It's a decision you make every day."

"I've known a lot of addicts in my life, but none that were sober. Working undercover for the ATF might've given me a skewed perception of drug abuse." His gaze grew distant, as if he was seeing something in his mind's eye. "When Oliver started using, I couldn't understand it. He had a football scholarship, excellent grades, a family that loved him. Yes, he struggled after his friend died in a car accident, but why throw his life away? It made me angry, and I didn't respond well."

"Don't be hard on yourself. There's not a guidebook to tell you how to navigate such a difficult situation." Megan's heart tightened at the pain in his voice. "Oliver loved you very much. Deep down, we both knew that what we were doing was wrong, but drugs got rid of the pain. It's an escape."

Jax tilted his head. "What were you escaping?"

"My mom died. That's why I moved to Knoxville to live with my grandparents. When I met Oliver, he understood me. We were both grieving. Drugs were a terrible way to cope, but neither of us understood the hurt we were causing to ourselves or others. Addiction changes your brain. It makes you lose sight of everything except your next fix." She handed him the empty cup before resting her head against the pillow. "What time is it?"

"Almost six."

"My grandparents will be here soon." Nana and Pops had rushed to the hospital the moment they learned Megan had been attacked. Once the doctor assured everyone she'd make a full recovery, Megan had convinced them to go home and get a few hours of sleep. "What are the chances they'll bring coffee?"

"I'd say better than average." Pops entered the room, carrying a tray of takeout coffees. His thick gray beard and full head of hair gave him a rugged, lumberjack look, especially paired with the flannel shirts he favored. Years ago, a nasty fall on a roofing job had left him with a slight limp, but nothing could diminish his steady strength.

He kissed Megan's forehead. "Hi, Ladybug." His gaze drifted to Jax and narrowed. "Detective."

There was no love lost between Clay Ingles and the Taylor family. Jax may have saved Megan's life last night, but her grandfather didn't consider that payment enough for all the pain their accusations had caused his granddaughter. Still, she appreciated the fact that Pops was cordial... even if it was grudgingly.

Nana bustled into the room on her husband's heels,

her silver hair soft and fluffed like a cloud, rosy cheeks flushed with the brisk morning air. She carried a tray covered with aluminum foil. Megan's mouth watered as the scent of yeasty bread filled the room. Rose Ingles had worked in a bakery for most of her career and, although she'd retired fifteen years ago, retained all her skills.

"I brought breakfast," Nana said. "Hope you're hungry."

"Starving." Megan wanted to weep with joy when her grandmother lifted the aluminum foil to reveal home-made kolaches. She'd missed dinner last night and, with the head injury, hadn't felt like eating much anyway. But now her hunger roared to life. It was probably why she was still nauseated.

Jax rose from his chair. "I'll step outside for a bit. Give you some time to talk."

"Not without a kolache you won't." Nana gave him a pointed look, her soft smile leaving no room for argument. Unlike Pops, she held no grudges against Jax or his family. She'd counseled Megan to be patient with the Taylor family, to be understanding of the painful loss they'd suffered, and to forgive their need to throw misplaced blame on her shoulders.

Nana handed Jax a kolache wrapped in a napkin before turning to her husband. "Clay, give Jax his coffee, please."

Pops grumbled under his breath but complied, holding the cup out stiffly.

Jax took it with a nod. "Thank you, sir." He lifted the wrapped kolache and tipped his head in Nana's direction. "Ma'am." His gaze finally landed on Megan and his tone was soft as he said, "If you need anything, I'll be right outside the door."

Her heart inexplicably skipped a beat. Before she could think much of it, Jax was already halfway across the room.

As soon as the door clicked shut behind him, Pops let out a frustrated sigh. "How long is he going to be hanging around for? I appreciate that Chief Garcia is taking these threats seriously, but I don't trust that fellow. He's caused us a lot of grief over the last few months."

"He saved my life, Pops." She gave her grandfather a knowing look. "I think that wipes the slate clean."

Pops grunted in reply. Then he handed Megan her coffee, his gaze sharp and unwavering. "That reminds me. I thought we were done keeping secrets from each other, Ladybug. Why didn't you tell us about the threatening emails you'd been receiving?"

Nana shot him a warning look. "Now, Clay—"

"No, Nana. Pops is right." Megan hated to disappoint her grandparents. She'd done it far too often. "I'm sorry. I should've told you about the emails weeks ago, but I didn't want to worry you."

Her grandfather's posture eased, the hardness in his eyes softening to something closer to hurt. "Keeping us in the dark doesn't stop us from worrying about you. It only hurts our feelings. Family takes care of each other."

It was a motto he lived by. And it wasn't just words. When Megan's mother died of a sudden heart attack, her paternal grandparents had taken in a terrified and lost teenager without a whisper of complaint. Megan had repaid their love and support by rebelling. It was only after getting clean that she realized what a treasure her grandparents truly were. They were all the family she had left, and the only connection she had to her biological father who'd died when Megan was a baby.

Warmth flooded through her as Nana wrapped an arm around her shoulders. "We love you, honey. I'm so glad you're okay."

"I love you too." Megan's voice wavered as the reality of what had almost happened last night finally sank into her.

A knock interrupted the moment. Megan quickly swiped at the tear running down her cheek as Chief Garcia entered. His uniform was rumpled—probably from working most of the night—and the shadows under his eyes resembled bruises. Still, he offered Clay and Rose a warm smile and shook both of their hands before turning his attention to Megan. "How are you feeling?"

"Better. Thank you." The coffee and her grandmother's homemade kolache had eased her headache. She adjusted the blankets around her waist, feeling slightly embarrassed to be speaking to the chief while wearing a hospital gown. A silly thing, considering she'd nearly been killed last night, but still...

Nana, ever perceptive, reached into a bag and pulled out a shawl. Megan gratefully wrapped it around her shoulders while her grandfather offered the chief one of Nana's kolaches.

Chief Garcia swallowed it down in three bites,

finishing the quick meal off with a bottle of water. "Thank you kindly, Clay. I haven't eaten since dinner and that was a long time ago." He tossed the empty bottle in the trash and wiped his mouth with a napkin. "I'm sorry to drop in so early this morning, but I have a few questions, Megan. Feel up to answering them?"

"Of course. Whatever I can do to help." She wanted the man who'd assaulted her found as soon as possible.

"How many people have keys to your vehicle?"

"I have two sets. One I carry with me and the spare stays at home." She frowned. "Why?"

He ignored her question. "Do you know if the spare set is accounted for?"

"It is," Clay said. "I saw it on the hook this morning when I went to get my car keys."

The chief nodded. "I figured as much, but needed to be sure." He pulled out a pad from his front pocket and scribbled a note. "We believe the man who attacked you last night used a device to bypass your security alarm and unlock your vehicle. Normally, criminals use them to steal vehicles, but this time, it was to sneak inside and lie in wait. I'm deeply concerned this was a planned assault."

"It's the same man who wrote all those emails, isn't it?" Clay demanded. "He's out to hurt Megan."

"We haven't definitively linked the emails to the attack, but logic would dictate they're probably connected." Chief Garcia focused back on Megan. "I know I asked you this last night, but witnesses sometimes remember details after they've had time to process things.

Are you sure there wasn't anything familiar about the man who attacked you?"

Megan tightened her hold on the shawl and shook her head. "No, sir."

"Have you had a run-in with anyone lately that made you uncomfortable? Had a confrontation with someone in town?"

She breathed out. "No, sir. I get whispers and funny looks from time to time—especially since the investigation into Oliver's accident was reopened—but that's normal. Knoxville's a small town and people gossip. But no one has been aggressive or directly hostile."

"What about Wesley Taylor?"

Megan blinked in surprise. "Oliver's twin? Does he even live in town? Last I heard, he was in the military."

"He moved back around nine months ago." The chief frowned, keeping his gaze locked on her. "I take it you didn't know that?"

"No." She fiddled with the fringe of the shawl. "The last time I saw Wesley was at Oliver's funeral. He told me to leave the church and stay away from his family." She swallowed, the sting of that moment still sharp after all these years. "I haven't seen him since."

Nana placed a comforting hand on Megan's shoulder. "Do you think Wesley has something to do with this, Chief?"

He didn't answer. Instead, he pulled a plastic evidence bag from his coat pocket. Inside was a photograph. "This was found near the lake. Do you recognize it, Megan?"

Megan took the bag from his outstretched hand. It was an old photo, worn and ripped on both sides, as if it'd been handled too many times. Oliver was on the left, young and carefree. His mop of dark hair was mussed, and he wore a football jersey. To his right were his twin, Wesley, and a younger Jax. The brothers were happy, arms wrapped around each other, caught in mid-laugh. The background was blurry and hard to distinguish.

"I've never seen this picture before." She looked up at Chief Garcia. "Jax is in the photo. Have you asked him?"

"Yes, right before I spoke to you. He thinks it was taken just before he left for college, shortly after Oliver's sixteenth birthday."

"I wasn't living in Knoxville then. Oliver and I became friends after I moved here during my senior year." Confusion set in. "I'm sorry, you found this near the lake? So you think the attacker dropped it?"

"Possibly. It was discovered in the area where you and the attacker tussled."

Megan shuddered, remembering the sheer terror of being yanked out from beneath the bush by her ankle. It was by the grace of God she'd survived.

"Have you spoken to Wesley?" Clay asked, his tone sharp and protective. "What does he say about this?"

The chief's jaw tightened. "Officers went to his cabin but could not locate him."

Silence hung heavy in the room. Megan's mind spun. Wesley had never liked her—and she couldn't blame him. Megan had been an integral part of Oliver's drug days, a bad influence that led to his twin's death. But why come after her now? It'd been ten years.

Then again, Wesley hadn't been living in town until recently. Had he decided it was time to get revenge?

"I know you're all worried," Chief Garcia said, his expression both serious and understanding, "but my department is working hard to solve this case. What I don't want is for assumptions to be made based on my questions or this photograph. Wesley is innocent until proven guilty. He may have nothing to do with this."

Megan prayed that was the case. The emails were chilling. The attack, terrifying. Being assaulted by a stranger was bad enough, but that someone from the Taylor family—someone Oliver had loved and trusted—wanted her dead? It was far more personal. And more dangerous. The attacker hadn't acted on impulse. He'd planned the assault carefully, which meant he might try again.

And that thought shook her to the core.

SIX

Jax pounded on the front door of his brother's cabin. The rough wood shook with the force of his efforts. "Wesley, open up!"

Silence was the only answer. Birds flitted through tree branches overhead, their joyful songs a stark contrast to Jax's own turmoil. He hadn't slept in almost twenty-four hours. Chief Garcia had stationed an officer outside Megan's hospital room so that Jax could go home and rest. Instead, he'd driven straight to Wesley's house.

He needed answers, and he needed them now.

Worry fueled his steps as he circled the log cabin. The building was constructed out of electrical poles, notched together in perfect alignment and sealed with a mixture of cement and clay. A solar panel gleamed on the roof. Barrels nestled in the grass collected rainwater. Wesley lived off the grid. This property had once belonged to their grandparents and was used for hunting. There wasn't a neighbor for miles.

Jax peeked into the small window on the side of the cabin. His brother hadn't bothered with curtains. The one-room house was tidy. Dishes sat in the drying rack on the narrow kitchen counter. A handmade table, a rocking chair, and a bed were the only pieces of furniture. Books were piled on the floor. The fireplace was dark, but ashes showed it'd been used at some point. He pushed off from the house and continued around back. A generator sat hunched in an alcove. It was silent.

Jax touched the metal. Ice-cold. His brother hadn't been here recently. His beat-up Ford truck was also missing, along with the small motorized dinghy he used for fishing. Normally, Wesley's disappearances weren't cause for concern. Since being discharged from the military, he'd hidden away in the cabin, preferring solitude to people. He'd also take off for days at a time. Hunting. Fishing. Sometimes just hiking. Anything that kept him outdoors and away from others.

The attack on Megan, however, changed things. Jax didn't believe Wesley was responsible, but he was concerned that his brother wouldn't have a good explanation for where he was during the time in question. And then there was the photograph... why would Megan's attacker have a picture of Oliver and his brothers?

Jax sucked in a breath of pine-scented air and breathed it out slowly. He couldn't let fear take his mind down dark paths. Instead, he lifted his gaze toward the sky. "God, I need your help. I'm worried."

Jax had practically raised Oliver and Wesley. Their father worked on oil rigs and was gone for most of their childhood. Their mother was a factory worker, sometimes taking double shifts to make ends meet. The bond forged between the boys ran deep. Jax hadn't realized how deep until Oliver was gone, and by then, it was too late to correct all of his mistakes.

He marched back to his SUV and fired up the engine. With a last look at his brother's cabin, Jax headed back to town. An hour later, he pulled into his parents' cracked driveway. His childhood home was better taken care of these days now that his mom and dad were both retired and had the extra time. New shutters, an updated roof, and plants in the flowerbeds brightened the exterior.

He entered without knocking, calling out a hello to announce his presence. His mom exited the kitchen, wiping her hands on a dishtowel, a smile brightening her face. "Isn't this a surprise?" She offered her cheek for a kiss and then studied his face. Her smile wilted. "What's wrong?"

"We need to have a family meeting. Where's Dad?"

"In the kitchen."

Jax followed her into the sunny room. His father was seated at the worn table tucked in the breakfast nook, a discarded plate resting at his elbow, the remnants of eggs lingering on the porcelain. Deep worry lines marched across his face and his mouth was a stern slash. Greg Taylor had never been a joyful man, but years of hard labor and the death of one of his sons had drained the last wisp of happiness from him. Jax couldn't remember the last time he'd seen his dad smile.

"Coffee, *mijo*?" Valentina handed Jax a cup of coffee

before swiping a stray hair away from her forehead. Silver strands wove through her jet-black hair, but she was still a striking woman. Every one of her sons favored her in looks, down to the curve of their nose and the olive skin tone. Personality-wise, though, the Taylor men were famous for their fiery tempers and protective nature. Those were inherited from their dad.

"Mamacita, sit down, please." Jax pulled out a chair for his mother. He didn't want her bustling around the kitchen, pushing food at him during this conversation. Then he claimed the chair next to her. "Have you heard from Wesley? I need to know where he is."

"Why are you looking for your brother?" Greg's frown deepened as his gaze narrowed.

Jax hesitated. His family would hear about what happened one way or another. It was far better for him to break the news, but he didn't relish doing it. "Megan Ingles was attacked last night and nearly killed."

Beside him, Valentina gasped.

Greg's frown deepened. "What does Wesley..." The implication must've hit him because his nostrils suddenly flared, as red blotches appeared in his cheeks. "That woman—" He spat the word as if it was a swear. "—can't leave us in peace. It's bad enough she killed Oliver, now she's accusing Wesley of attacking her."

Jax held up a hand to ward off his father's rant. "She didn't accuse Wesley of anything. There's evidence that suggests someone tried to kill her to avenge Oliver's death. The chief wants to talk to Wesley just to clear him from the suspect list, but he's missing."

"So what? Wesley didn't do it."

"You and I both know that, but the chief still needs to talk to him." Jax's gaze flickered to his mother. "If you know where he is, please tell me. The faster we clear this up, the better it is for everyone."

Valentina shook her head. "I haven't spoken to him since last week. Have you tried his cell phone?"

Jax nodded. "It's turned off." Another thing Wesley often did when he wanted to escape the world. Not unusual for his brother, but given the circumstances, it made him look guiltier. "His truck is gone, and so is his fishing boat. Officers have checked with the local bait shops. Wesley hasn't been by recently."

"He likes to visit different spots," Valentina said, concern furrowing her brows. "New ones. He could be gone for days." She paused. "What evidence did they find to make them believe Wesley is behind the attack on Megan?"

"I can't share that with you. It's an active investigation."

"Unbelievable." Greg pounded the table with his fist. "Oliver was killed and the police do nothing. Absolutely nothing. They let his killer walk free for years. Now that she's been attacked, it's suddenly important to figure out what happened. Well, let me tell you, if a friend or neighbor took matters into their own hands and got justice for Oliver... well, I'd like to shake that person's hand and say thanks."

Jax stared, stunned by his father's callousness. He understood his anger, but vigilante justice wasn't the answer. "Attacking Megan is a crime. Whoever is responsible for this will be caught and prosecuted."

His dad grew redder. "I can't believe you're defending her."

"I'm not defending her. I'm standing up for what's right."

"What's right?" Greg rose from his seat. "Is it right that I had to bury my son? Is it right that she caused the accident that killed him and gets to go on living the rest of her life without being punished?"

Getting this worked up was bad for his dad's weak heart. Jax held up his hands in the classic sign of surrender, hoping to calm his father's anger. "Of course not. I'm sorry. I don't mean to upset you—"

"You've disappointed me. That's what you've done." Greg jabbed a finger at him. "You promised to look into the accident, to get justice for your brother, but you haven't done anything."

Valentina stepped between them. "That's enough, Greg." Her tone brooked no argument. The only time their mother ever stood up to their father was in defense of her children. "Jax isn't to blame here. He's trying to help Wesley."

"He has a strange way of doing it."

Greg turned and stormed out, slamming the back door behind him so hard that the dishes in the cupboards rattled.

Valentina winced and then turned her sympathetic gaze toward Jax. She placed her thin hands on his shoulders and kissed the top of his head. "I'm sorry, *mi amor*. He's angry and doesn't know what he's saying."

Guilt mingled with worry in a toxic swirl, eating away at Jax's stomach. His dad's accusations weren't true. He'd spent hundreds of hours poring over the case file. No one wanted Oliver's killer brought to justice more than Jax did, but he couldn't manufacture evidence out of thin air.

He told himself it didn't matter. The relationship with his dad had always been a complicated one, filled with responsibility and expectations, but that didn't stop the deep hurt in his heart. The way his father had looked at him... like he was a disappointment. It mirrored everything Jax thought of himself.

He'd failed Oliver. Jax had been in college, determined to live his own life, when his younger brother began floundering. The drugs... the recklessness... the lies and the secrets... perhaps all of it could have been prevented if Jax had prioritized his family over himself. Instead, he'd been selfish, and it had cost him dearly.

He wouldn't make the same mistake.

Jax rose from the chair and kissed his mother's cheek. "Please tell me if you hear from Wesley."

Valentina nodded, but concern clouded her features. She held onto his arm. "What are you going to do?"

"I'm going to prove Wesley didn't do this."

SEVEN

A stiff wind whipped through Megan's hair as she hit the fob to lock her grandfather's Cadillac. Her vehicle was still being held as evidence, although Chief Garcia hoped to have it back to her within the week. The parking lot attached to Clearview Counseling was packed. Mondays were always busy. Megan could have taken more time off from work, but she'd spent the weekend sequestered in her house and was on the verge of going stir-crazy. Sitting around gave her far too much time to think. Nana had tried distracting her with Hallmark movies, but they hadn't kept Megan's mind from turning over the attack again and again.

Chief Garcia had increased patrols in her neighborhood over the weekend and, so far, everything had remained quiet. Wesley was still missing though. Megan had spent far too many hours turning over his potential involvement in her mind. She couldn't sit around anymore and think about things that weren't within her control. She needed to feel useful. To serve others. Going to work was the best medicine.

But first caffeine.

The rich scent of coffee hung in the crisp air. Megan hauled her laptop bag over her shoulder and hurried across the parking lot to Roasted Beans. The bright yellow awning was a spot of cheer against the heavy cast of clouds in the sky. A sign on the sidewalk announced the daily special: a cinnamon roll and a latte.

Bells over the door announced her arrival. Several tables were occupied, and the hum of conversation filled the space. A barista behind the counter glanced up but remained focused on filling orders. "Welcome in. What can I get you?"

Megan scanned the glass display case, where cinnamon rolls dripped with luscious icing. Her mouth watered. "I'll have the daily special," she said, using the wallet app on her phone to pay. Then she moved to join a small group of people waiting for their orders at the other end of the counter.

It didn't take long for the whispers to start.

A woman standing near the pastry case leaned toward her companion, speaking in a low voice but loud enough for Megan to catch snippets. "That's her... the girl who was mixed up in that accident years ago. You know, Oliver Taylor..."

Her companion cast a glance in Megan's direction, then glanced away. "Didn't she—?"

"Yeah. And now she's involved in some kind of trouble again. She was attacked Friday night."

Megan's cheeks burned, and she tried to focus on the cheerful chalkboard menu above the counter, willing herself to ignore the stares and whispers. She knew this would happen—Knoxville was small enough that word traveled fast, but big enough that not everyone knew her personally. That didn't stop them from speculating.

Behind her, someone muttered, "She should've stayed gone. Troublemaker."

Megan's grip tightened on the strap of her laptop bag. There was nothing she could say. People would believe what they wanted, just like they had ten years ago. She wasn't that lost teenager anymore, but small towns had long memories.

"Daily special—latte and cinnamon roll!" The barista's cheerful voice cut through the tension, giving Megan a reason to move. She grabbed her order, muttered a quick thank-you, and made her way to the exit. The bells jingled as someone yanked open the door. Megan stopped short just before plowing into the large man entering the coffee shop.

"Quinton." Surprise made her voice unnaturally high. She cleared her throat and forced a smile for the Clearview Counseling client. "Hi."

Broad and stocky, Quinton Jones was a former body-builder who'd abused steroids and other drugs to bulk up. He'd been arrested for assault and was court ordered to complete drug rehab and therapy sessions as part of his plea agreement. Megan wasn't his therapist—her friend and colleague, Douglas O'Neal was—but she knew most of the patients that came into their office by name. The friendly and relaxed atmosphere at Clearview helped clients feel at ease.

Recognition flashed across his meaty features and then Quinton's gaze slid away from her. "Are you a killer?"

The question shocked her. Around them, the hum of the coffee shop dimmed, as though the world had heard Quinton's words. Megan knew he didn't mean to be hurtful—he wasn't like that. Social cues weren't his strength, and he often said things others would tiptoe around. Still, the bluntness of his question hit her like a slap.

"I—" Megan faltered, her voice catching in her throat. The curious stares from nearby tables prickled her skin. "No, Quinton. I'm not a killer."

"People say you murdered someone. They talk about it a lot." He frowned. "So are they lying?"

She hated this. Hated that the shadow of her past followed her around constantly. Megan's hand tightened on the coffee in her hand, but the warmth seeping through the paper cup did nothing to ease the block of ice lodged in her chest.

Douglas O'Neal, her friend and coworker, appeared at her side. He was dressed for work in a sweater and slacks, his reddish-brown hair artfully rumpled, a half-drunk coffee in one hand. His laptop was tucked under the other arm. She hadn't noticed him earlier, but there were a few tables in the back. Douglas often came to the coffee shop to answer emails before heading to the office.

"Good morning, Quinton." Douglas shot Megan a

sympathetic glance before focusing back on his client. He'd obviously overheard some of the exchange and was coming to her rescue. "How's everything going?"

Quinton's shoulders relaxed a notch. "I was getting some coffee before our meeting. I saw Megan."

"Good call on the coffee. It's cold out there. Try the daily special. The cinnamon rolls shouldn't be missed." Douglas's voice was cheerful and disarming. He placed a reassuring hand on Megan's back, steering her toward the door. "See you in half an hour, Quinton."

The slap of crisp air was a welcome relief to her heated cheeks. She fell into step beside Douglas as they crossed the parking lot to their office. "Thanks for saving me back there. Quinton's questions caught me off guard." She snorted. "I don't know why. He only said what everyone else is thinking."

"Not everyone." Douglas slanted a glance her way. "I'm sure at least one or two people in there were discussing the secret ingredient in the cinnamon rolls or whether the barista is dating that new guy working at the hardware store. You know, important stuff."

Megan couldn't help but laugh. "Critical town matters."

"Exactly." His smile dimmed a bit as concern clouded his features. "I know it's hard when they talk about you, but chin up, Megs. People will move on to something else soon enough."

Megs. Her old nickname from high school. She'd known Douglas back then, but they hadn't been close. Since moving back and coming to work at Clearview

Counseling, however, their friendship had grown. While Douglas saw all kinds of clients, he specialized in bullied teenagers. His kindness and compassion were born out of his own experiences in school. If anyone knew how difficult it was to be the brunt of gossip, it was Douglas.

"You're right." Megan had run away from her problems last time, but now she refused to. Nana's bout with cancer last year had been a valuable wake-up call. She didn't have forever with her grandparents. Knoxville was their home, and she'd endured a lot more painful things than mere gossip. "Thanks for being such a good friend, Douglas."

His smile was warm as he held open the office door for her. "Anytime, Megs."

Megan crossed the threshold into the small reception area. The soft gray walls and leather couches were both warm and professional. Thick carpeting muffled her footsteps as she made small talk with Douglas about his weekend until he veered off to his office. Megan's was at the end of the building. She sipped her coffee, happy to discover it'd cooled to the perfect temperature.

Tess Gates, her boss, spotted Megan walking by and waved her into the conference room. The table was covered with paperwork.

"Morning." Tess rose. Her black hair was arranged in thick braids that twisted into a topknot. The lime-colored suit played off her skin tone, making her appear younger than her fifty-three years. A pencil was tucked behind one ear, and she smiled gently. "I'm glad to see you."

Megan leaned over and glimpsed financial spreadsheets. "Please tell me you don't need help with the books. Math was never my forte."

Tess laughed. "No. Don't worry. I wouldn't wish bookkeeping on my worst enemy." Her expression softened. "I know we already spoke this morning, but if you need to take a break or leave early, just say so. We can cover your clients."

"Thank you." The supportive atmosphere was the thing Megan loved best about Clearview. Tess was the best boss she'd ever had. Conscientious, empathetic, and responsible. It was understandable after the assault that she'd want to make sure Megan was in the right headspace to see clients. "I'll let you know if it gets to be too much. I promise."

She chatted a few more minutes with Tess before heading for her office. The moment she entered the room, with its soft blue chairs and the wide-oak desk, the stress leached from her shoulders. Outside the world might be chaos, but here... in this space, she had purpose.

A quick glance at her watch confirmed she had fifteen minutes before her first client arrived. Enough time to sort through her inbox. She fired up her laptop, sipping her latte while the system booted. Seconds later, she was reviewing her emails. Megan froze as she scrolled through the messages flooding her screen. Dozens of them. The time and date stamps showed they'd been coming all weekend. All from the same sender, the subject line in all caps.

IT'S NOT OVER. NEXT TIME, I WILL KILL YOU.

EIGHT

Hours later, Megan said goodbye to the last client of the day and then dropped into her desk chair. The building was quiet, since most of the staff had left thirty minutes ago. Weariness sank into her. The constant string of appointments had kept her mind away from the latest threatening emails, but now that the hustle of the day had faded, worry crept in. She opened her laptop and a string of new messages loaded. Thankfully, none were from her stalker.

Megan pulled a tattered Bible from her desk drawer. Page markers and bookmarks littered the pages. She opened to one of her favorite verses and read aloud, "So do not fear, for I am with you; do not be dismayed, for I am your God. I will strengthen you and help you; I will uphold you with my righteous right hand."

The words soothed her. She touched the handwritten note in the margin, feeling the indentation of the words on the page. *You are never alone. God is always with you.*

The message had been written decades ago by her father. Megan had never known him. He'd died before she was born in a military training accident, but having his Bible, reading his handwritten notes in the margins, provided a connection she cherished.

A knock on her open doorframe jerked her head up. Jax stood in the doorway. A tan blazer hugged his broad shoulders and his jaw was clean-shaven, but his slacks were wrinkled, as if he'd been wearing them for hours. His badge hung from his belt. Exhaustion and stress had added worry lines to the corners of his mouth, and shadows lingered under his piercing blue eyes.

"Sorry to intrude." His gaze dropped to the Bible in her hands. "The receptionist said I could come straight back." He hesitated. "I could wait if you need a few minutes."

"No, it's okay." She waved him in. Nerves jittered her insides. She'd reported the latest emails to Noah this morning but hadn't heard anything back yet. To her knowledge, Wesley was still missing. "I was just..." Megan touched her father's note in the margin of the Bible. "Reminding myself that God is always watching over me."

"Noah told me about the latest emails."

Megan nodded. "Has there been any progress in finding out who sent them?"

"Penelope, our cyber specialist, tried tracing the origin, but whoever sent the emails was smart enough to filter them through a virtual private network. We can't identify who sent them or where they were sent from."

Jax crossed to the window and gazed out on Main Street. It was bustling with traffic, despite the gloomy weather and frigid temperatures. "Technicians are still going through your Toyota, but so far, they've come up empty-handed. No fingerprints. No DNA other than yours. We haven't found any witnesses who saw someone breaking into your vehicle. None of the cameras on Main Street capture a view of your workplace parking lot. We can't identify the boat the attacker used to escape. The only lead we have at the moment is the photograph dropped during the tussle with you."

The photograph of Oliver with his brothers. Megan had spent a fair share of time over the weekend thinking about that too. "Were you able to trace when the picture was taken?"

He turned to face her. "I went through my mom's photo albums. As best I can tell, it was during my last trip home before graduating from college. I've been racking my brain trying to pinpoint the day, but the timeline doesn't match any of the weekend games Oliver played. It's probably from an after-school practice."

"Then it was definitely taken before I knew Oliver. When I met him, he had already stopped playing football." She paused, then gently asked, "Have you spoken to Wesley?"

"No one knows where he is. My parents are calling up family members and soldiers he served with, but I doubt anything will come of it. Wesley goes off the grid from time to time." Jax circled the chair and pointed to the Bible, still resting open on her desk. "May I?"

Surprised, she handed it to him. He read the high-lighted verse she'd been reading and then flipped through the pages. "I've always been fond of Ephesians 4:25." Jax set the Bible on the desk, turned toward her, and tapped on the page. "Therefore each of you must put off false-hood, and speak truthfully to your neighbor, for we are all one body."

Megan's gaze lifted to his. His expression was hard and unyielding, nothing like the man who'd been so kind to her in the hospital after the assault. This was the Jax she was familiar with—untrusting and wary.

Her heart skipped a beat. "What's going on, Jax?"

"I need you to be honest with me."

She straightened to her full height, letting conviction bleed into her voice. "I have been."

He didn't bat an eyelash, didn't look away. "Someone ran you and Oliver off the road on the night of the accident?" He tapped the Bible again with his finger. "You swear it. As a Christian. As Oliver's friend."

"Yes." Megan held his gaze, praying he was open-minded enough to listen this time. "I've made mistakes, Jax. Lots of them. Not telling the truth about what happened that night right away was one of them. I was scared. Oliver was high and paranoid, and a lot of what he said didn't make sense, but he was convinced someone was out to kill him. Then we were run off the road. I was terrified whoever was after Oliver would come for me next. It took days for me to share what had happened to Pops and my sponsor. They convinced me to revise my statement, but by then, no one believed me. I—"

Tears lodged in her throat, and it took a second to swallow them back down. "I cared about Oliver. It haunts me that my mistakes—my falsehoods—are the reason his killer is still out there. I'm deeply sorry for everything that happened. I wish..."

She wished for a lot of things. The what-ifs were difficult to live with. She should've worked harder to convince Oliver to get clean. Or ignored the speed limit that night and arrived five minutes earlier to pick him up. Or somehow been a better driver when they were rammed.

Most of all, she wished Oliver was still alive.

Her chin trembled. "I'd do anything to change what happened."

Jax's gaze scanned her face, as if searching for any sign of deception. Then the hard mask hiding his emotions disappeared and a pain she'd never seen before darkened his eyes. "Me too."

Her heart shattered at the devastation in his voice, and for the first time, Megan understood she wasn't the only who blamed themselves for Oliver's death. She struggled to find any words that might bring him comfort. "Jax..."

"I need your help." He turned away and paced the length of the office. "Chief Garcia believes my brother is responsible for the threatening emails and the attack on you, but Wesley wouldn't do this. Yes, he's struggled since being discharged from the military. He's more secretive now. More reclusive. But he's not a murderer."

Megan wasn't sure whether to argue with Jax. She

also wanted to believe Wesley was innocent, but the photograph found at the scene of the attack, along with his disappearance, was concerning. "It's not uncommon for soldiers to suffer from PTSD or have issues readjusting to civilian life."

She'd counseled several former military members who'd abused drugs or alcohol to cope with trauma. "Wesley may not be thinking clearly. Oliver was his twin. They loved each other deeply, and it wouldn't surprise me to learn that Wesley blames me for his brother's death. Anger and grief can twist into a need for vengeance."

Jax stopped his pacing and faced her. "I know, but it still doesn't add up, Megan. Wesley's a trained Navy SEAL. Logistically, he would've planned for every contingency. He would've struck without warning. Wesley wouldn't have sent dozens of threatening emails beforehand. He certainly wouldn't have been sloppy enough to drop an incriminating photograph."

Megan turned that over in her mind and realized there was logic in his arguments. "What are you suggesting? That someone is framing your brother?"

"It sounds farfetched, but it's the only reasonable explanation." He planted his hands on the back of her visitor's chair. "Oliver told you someone was trying to kill him. Then you were run off the road. Right after the accident, when you came clean about what happened, no one believed you. That may have saved your life."

Goosebumps rose on her arms. She'd had nightmares about Oliver's killer coming after her. That fear had been a large part of the reason she'd fled Knoxville ten years ago. Still, it didn't seem reasonable for the killer to come after her now. "I've already told the police everything I know. Why send threatening emails and try to kill me ten years later?"

Jax met her gaze. "Because I insisted the case be reopened. As the lead investigator, Noah has been reviewing the evidence. He believed your version of events and wanted to pursue new suspects."

Shock rendered her speechless. She'd prayed someone in law enforcement would believe her, that Oliver's actual killer would be caught, but it never seemed likely. Coupled with the gossip and rumors running through town about her... well, Megan hadn't been sure she'd had any friends at all. Emotion clogged her throat. "Noah believed me?"

Jax nodded. "He argued with me the night you came to the police station to tell us about the emails." His gaze dropped from hers and landed on the Bible, still sitting on her desk. "He vouched for you as a friend. Said you were honorable and good. He also told me that if you'd caused Oliver's death, you would've taken responsibility for it. Even if it meant prison time."

Megan was almost struck dumb by the knowledge that Noah had defended her. She'd left that night thinking no one cared. She'd been wrong. And it was a relief to realize her own assessment of Noah as a person and a law enforcement officer had been right.

Maybe she could trust her instincts after all.

"He's right." Megan waited until Jax's gaze lifted to

hers and then continued, "I would've taken responsibility. I know it's not hard evidence or solid proof, but I hope you believe me."

Once again, he studied her expression and then he nodded. "I do. And I'm sorry. If I hadn't insisted that you were guilty of negligent homicide, Noah might've figured out you were telling the truth earlier and expanded the investigation. If I'd been more open-minded... shoot, if I'd just stayed out of Noah's way and let him do his job..." Heat crept into his cheeks. "We wouldn't be here now."

Megan couldn't let him take all the blame. He was stubborn, yes, but he was also grieving the loss of his brother. And her initial lies had made her an unreliable witness. She shook her head. "No, Jax. We both made mistakes. The question is how do we move forward from here? Do you really think Oliver's killer is coming after me now?"

"You're a witness, Megan. A loose end. And like I said, Noah was prepared to pursue new leads. I don't know if the killer knows that, or if he was just scared. But I think Oliver's murderer will do anything to ensure he stays out of prison." His jaw hardened. "And whoever it is hates my family enough to frame Wesley for the crime."

"So the emails... the photograph..."

"They're a ruse designed to send the police on a wild goose chase after my brother."

Megan's mind whirled. She didn't want to believe that someone could be diabolical enough to create such an elaborate scheme, but the man who'd attacked her was smart and daring. Could Jax be right? A chill raced down her spine.

She fought against her emotions, approaching the situation from a logical perspective. "Whoever is behind this would have to know Wesley was planning a trip." She paused. "Unless you think..." She didn't want to put words to the horrifying notion that'd popped into her mind.

Jax shook his head. "No, I don't think the killer has attacked Wesley. A few people in town knew he was taking a trip, and there's no sign of a struggle in his house. Clothes, camping equipment, fishing gear, and his rifle are missing from his house. His truck and boat are also gone. More than likely, he's in the wilderness somewhere, completely unaware that someone is framing him for murder."

Megan let out the breath she'd been holding. "Well, that's a relief. Wesley doesn't have a cell?"

"He has a satellite phone, which he left turned off and sitting in his house." He scraped a hand through his hair. "Wesley is used to being out of touch with our family for extended periods of time while on deployment. This isn't the first time he's gone dark since returning home. Before it was always an annoyance. Now, it's a serious problem."

Worry radiated from him. Megan circled the desk, the natural need to comfort a hurting person instinctive. "He'll come back. And once he talks to Chief Garcia, this whole thing will be cleared up."

"Not necessarily. Wesley is in the middle of nowhere

by himself. He won't have a verifiable alibi." Jax breathed out. "That's why I need your help."

"What can I do?"

Before Jax could answer, Megan's cell phone rang. The special ringtone for her grandfather was exceedingly loud in the quiet office. "Excuse me." She crossed back to the desk, snatching up the device right before the call went to voicemail. "Hi, Pops."

"Thank God! Where are you, Megan?"

"I'm still at the office." Her heart rate jumped at the controlled panic in her grandfather's voice. "What's wrong?"

"Hold on."

His voice was muffled as he covered the phone and exchanged words with someone else. Megan could hear Nana speaking in the background. It sounded like they were coordinating something. "Pops, what's going on? Is Nana okay?" Her grandmother's health had been fragile since her bout with pneumonia a few months ago. "Pops?"

Her voice must've betrayed her growing sense of urgency, because Jax rose. He crossed the room on long strides. She met his questioning gaze and shook her head to show she didn't know what was happening. He placed a reassuring hand on her arm. His touch was warm and grounding.

"Pops, answer me." Her tone was sharp, so unlike the normal way she spoke to her grandfather, but Megan was struggling to keep the panic at bay.

"Your grandmother's fine," Pops finally said. "But...

never mind, I'll explain when I see you. Don't move from your office. Chief Garcia will send a patrol unit to pick you up."

She went cold. "What happened?"

"You got another message from your stalker."

NINE

Jax tightened his hold on the steering wheel as he maneuvered through an intersection, past a farm truck loaded with hay bales and a family sedan packed with kids dressed in karate uniforms. His turret lights strobed, alerting other drivers that he was in a rush, but he hadn't activated the siren since no one was in physical danger. At least, not at the moment. Megan's grandparents were fine. Officers were already at the house. Chief Garcia and Noah were en route.

For better or worse, the stalker was fixated on Megan. Whatever message he'd left was meant for her.

The road cleared, and Jax punched the gas harder. He spared a quick glance at his passenger. Megan sat stiffly, one hand gripping her purse, the other clutching the overhead roll bar. Her complexion was pale. Wisps of blonde hair covered the stitches in her scalp, and a faint bruise marred the delicate curve of her jaw. A thin cut etched across her top lip.

He'd made a terrible mistake.

Jax had been so fixated on blaming Megan for Oliver's death, he'd never considered the alternative—that she was telling the truth. His shortsightedness had cost him valuable investigation time and placed a target on her back. Questions crowded his mind, but one was more important than the others. "Who wanted Oliver dead?"

She gripped her purse tighter. "I don't know anything for certain."

His fingers flexed against the steering wheel and he shot her a warning look. "You and Oliver hadn't spoken in months, but you were friends. Good friends. For almost a year. You have a suspicion. I need to know who wanted Oliver dead. Who hates my family enough to kill one brother and frame another for a crime he didn't commit?"

"All I have are suspicions. A gut feeling. Before I share what I think, I need your word. As a Christian."

"Now's not the time for games."

"You're right. It isn't." Her gaze slanted his way and her eyes narrowed. "You're asking me to trust you. Until half an hour ago, you were convinced I'd killed Oliver. I refuse to toss a name to the police without some assurance that the person will be treated fairly."

Jax swallowed down his pride and his temper. Megan was right. After the way she'd been treated, it wasn't an unreasonable request. He gave a sharp nod. "You have my word. All I want is the truth."

She was quiet for a moment and then said, "Zeke Russell."

"Who is that?"

"Zeke and his brother, Cody, owned a gym called Bodybuilders. Zeke's the one who hooked Oliver into drugs, supplying him with oxy and steroids. Eventually, Oliver started fighting for Zeke in illegal competitions to pay for his habit. Their relationship was volatile. Sometimes violent. Zeke had a temper, and I suspect he was also abusing drugs."

"When you say violent, what do you mean exactly?"

Megan winced. "He threw a chair at Oliver once. Punched him in the face. I know there were other incidents, but those were the only ones I witnessed. Oliver put up with it because Zeke supplied him with drugs and paid him to fight in the competitions. It wasn't a friendship, per se, more like two men using each other. If Oliver did or said something that set Zeke off..." She shook her head. "I could see it going badly."

"When's the last time you saw or spoke to Zeke?" Jax slowed and turned into her tree-lined driveway. A patrol car was already in front of the house, but there was no sign of the officer who went with it.

"I cut everyone from that part of my life out when I got sober, Zeke included."

Jax opened his mouth to ask another question, but Megan was already out of the truck. She hurried to the front door. Sunshine picked up the red highlights in her hair and the tension riding her shoulders. The cab of his truck still carried the faint scent of her perfume, a faint vanilla that reminded him of warm cookies.

He quickly followed Megan into the house. She was

hugging her grandparents and the relief on the elderly couple's faces was clear. Officer Tucker Colburn also stood in the living room. His expression was grim, and he greeted Jax with a head nod.

"Report." Jax kept his voice low to prevent Megan and her grandparents from overhearing.

"Call came in at eighteen hundred hours. Clay Ingles and his wife returned from running errands and spotted an intruder on the property near the lake. They locked themselves in the house. I arrived on scene at eighteen-oh-seven and swept the property." Tucker's expression darkened. "Detective Graham arrived at eighteen-oh-nine. He was nearby and came to assist. The perpetrator was gone, but he left behind an explicit threat."

Jax glanced out the window and spotted his colleague Detective Dawson Graham walking near a dilapidated boathouse, partially shrouded by trees. Dressed in a hoodie and blue jeans, Dawson was off duty, but must've heard the call on the radio. He'd already roped off the area with yellow crime scene tape and was taking photographs. Whatever message the stalker had left wasn't visible from the house.

"How long were the Ingles out running errands?" Jax asked.

"About twenty minutes."

"Did they get a look at the trespasser?"

Tucker shook his head. "Not enough to identify him. Mr. Ingles said he saw a dark shadow down by the boathouse, but when he opened the back door to get a better look, the guy took off. He didn't follow because he was worried about leaving his wife alone in the house."

"Okay." Jax had more questions, but they could wait. "I'm going down to look."

Megan appeared at his side. "I'm coming with you."

"That's not a good idea." Clay stepped forward, a scowl creasing his mouth.

"Pops, I appreciate that you're trying to protect me, but it's unnecessary." She turned back to Jax. "I'll stay out of your way and do what you tell me to, but whatever is down there was left for me. I want to see it."

Her grandfather met Jax's gaze and gave a small shake of his head, his disapproval clear. Had Clay seen the message? Possibly. The old man was tough and didn't rattle easily. If he didn't want Megan to see the threat for herself, it must be bad.

Indecision warred within Jax. She was a civilian, and it would be a simple matter to bar her from the crime scene, but Megan had a point. The threat had been left for her. She had a right to see it.

Jax shot Clay an apologetic glance before nodding. "Okay, Megan. Let's go."

Megan followed him into the backyard. The property was secluded, the nearest neighbors hidden behind a dense wall of trees. Sunlight glinted off the lake. Ducks swam past, tucking themselves among the reeds close to the shore. It was peaceful and serene. But Jax's attention was drawn to the boathouse.

Unlike the rest of the property, the building perched next to the dock was battered and weathered. It listed to one side and was missing several boards from its north wall. "Do you use the boathouse for anything?"

"Just to store the lawn mower and tools. We don't own a boat."

Jax ducked under the crime scene tape, stopping Megan with a raised hand. "Wait here. Let me get a better sense of what we're dealing with before you come closer."

For a moment, it looked like she would argue, but then Megan nodded. "Okay."

Jax met Dawson near the entrance of the boathouse. His childhood friend greeted him with a head nod, his expression grim. Over six feet tall and built like an ox, Dawson cast a commanding shadow on the grass. A cowboy hat shaded his eyes, and despite wearing a bright orange hoodie with a tear along the pocket, he exuded a quiet confidence—the kind that came from a man who knew exactly where he belonged in the world.

"Bet this wasn't how you intended to spend your evening," Jax said in lieu of a greeting.

"Nope. I'm supposed to be fishing. Was headed to the north side of the lake when the call came in. Tucker was the closest patrol unit, but he was alone, and considering the attack on Megan a few days ago, I didn't think it was wise to leave him without backup."

Jax accepted the pair of gloves Dawson extended. "Where are the other patrols?"

"Handling a bar fight at The Broken Spur. An ugly one. Several wounded, three arrested."

"At six in the evening?" Jax shook his head. "Used to be people waited until midnight to act like fools."

"Lots of shift workers get off at two and start drinking. One guy thinks he's invincible after two beers, another's had a bad day at work and is looking to pick a fight, and suddenly you've got chairs flying and somebody's taking a whiskey bottle to the face." Dawson's gaze drifted to Megan, who was still standing near the crime scene tape. She'd forgotten her jacket in the house and stood with her arms crossed around her midsection. "What were you and Megan doing together?"

"Discussing the case. I'll fill you in later."

Dawson grunted. "I'm gonna hold you to that." He led the way around the side of the boathouse. "I've seen a lot of weird things, Jax, but this one is the freakiest. Whoever did this has a sick imagination."

Jax's steps faltered as he rounded the corner. A woman sat against the weathered wood of the boathouse, thick blonde hair obscuring her face. Slender. Dressed in slacks and a silk blouse. A high heel shoe hung awkwardly from one foot, the other lay in the grass. Drag marks disturbed the pine needles, leading from the lake to the boathouse, as if the body had been pulled from the shore. Blood coated her blouse, darkening the light blue fabric to a deep navy shade. A deep gash marred her neck.

It took far too many breaths to realize the woman wasn't real.

It was a mannequin.

"Holy..." Jax caught himself before an uncharacteristic curse slipped from his lips. "It looks just like Megan." He approached and crouched down. "From a distance, no one would know this wasn't a real person."

"Nearly gave her grandfather a heart attack. After we secured the property, he came out here before I could stop him."

No wonder Clay hadn't wanted Megan to come down to the boathouse. Jax didn't blame him. He scanned the tree line. "How did the perpetrator get on the property?"

"A boat." Dawson pointed to some smashed-down grass. "Slid the dinghy up on the shore over there, hauled the mannequin over to the boathouse, and arranged it. Mr. Ingles arrived and spotted someone down here just as the guy was finishing up. Then he took off."

An icy chill touched the back of Jax's neck. He didn't like this. Not one bit. "This took planning, but if he had the mannequin ready, it wouldn't have taken much time to set up."

"Agreed. A boat is the easiest way to get on and off the property. According to Mr. Ingles, he installed new deadbolts and a security system on the house yesterday, but hasn't hung the outside cameras." Dawson met Jax's gaze. "Megan's grandparents were only gone for twenty minutes. Either this guy got lucky and came when no one was home or he's been watching the house."

A buzzing, like a thousand bees, hummed overhead, interrupting their conversation. Jax recognized the sound of a drone. It wasn't unusual for amateur photographers to capture aerial shots of the lake, but this was private property. Federal law required drones to fly above four hundred feet, and this one sounded much lower.

Jax scanned the skyline, his nerves prickling. The buzzing was getting closer, but the drone wasn't visible.

Dawson turned, also scanning the sky. "A reporter?"

"Doubtful. They know better than this."

Still, Jax took off his jacket and draped it over the mannequin. They didn't need anyone taking a photograph of the crime scene.

The drone appeared over the tree line. Black legs extended and propellers whirring, it resembled a large flying bug. It dipped closer to the ground as it passed the boathouse. Jax squinted against the sunlight and raised a hand to shield his eyes. His heart stuttered.

A weapon was strapped to the drone's underside.

"Gun!" he shouted to Dawson, just as a stream of fire shot from the drone. Heat scorched the air, singeing the skin on Jax's face as the boathouse roof erupted into flames. Dawson dove to the ground and rolled for cover. The drone ignored him, swiveling toward the house.

Toward Megan.

She stood motionless in the yard, her mouth open in shock. Wind rifled her blonde hair. She was exposed, a perfect target. Jax yanked his weapon from its holster and took aim at the drone.

Fired.

Missed.

The drone adjusted course, zeroing in on Megan. Jax yelled her name, and for a moment, their gazes locked. He ran toward her, but the distance was insurmountable.

He wouldn't get close enough to shoot the drone down before it reached Megan. His chest tightened as he pushed his legs to move faster.

Megan took a step back as the flamethrower swung toward her. Terror flashed across her beautiful features. Then she turned and bolted for the trees.

Away from the house, away from her grandparents.

The drone whirled in pursuit, spitting a fresh stream of fire straight at Megan's retreating figure.

TEN

A burst of heat kissed Megan's back, and she yelped in fear. Her heart pounded against her rib cage. She pushed her legs to move faster, the uneven ground threatening to trip her at every step.

The buzzing behind her grew louder, and she knew the drone was gaining ground. Desperate to make herself a harder target to hit, she zigzagged toward the trees surrounding her property. They wouldn't provide her with a shred of protection. Once the flamethrower set the branches ablaze, even with the rain they'd had, it wouldn't take long for the fire to spread. She couldn't outrun a wildfire any more than she could escape the drone.

Her mind whirled, panic and fear making her thoughts frenetic. The relentless buzz of the drone stole her focus. Another blast of heat burst behind her, close enough to singe her hair. Her foot slipped on a patch of mud, and she went down hard, her knees hitting the ground with a bone-jarring thud. Pain shot up her legs and into her hips.

The drone zipped past. It rose into the sky and then spun, pointing the flamethrower's barrel straight at her.

Oh God, help me.

Megan scrambled to her feet, legs trembling from the fall and the exertion. She heard Jax shout her name, his voice raw with urgency, but with her breath ragged and the drone closing in, her sole focus was on survival. The fall had changed her direction. Instead of being trapped between the house and the forest, she was facing the back of the property. Like a beacon of hope, the lake glittered in the fading sunlight.

Megan raced for it. The drone followed in pursuit. Her boots pounded against the earth, then thudded on the dock as she sprinted down its length. Sweat coated her skin. There was no time to think about how cold the water would be or to register the searing cramp in her side. Death followed her. The drone's ever-present buzzing grew deafening. The flames at her back were so close she could feel the heat licking her skin.

With a last burst of energy, Megan leaped into the lake.

Cold darkness swallowed her whole. The icy water shocked her system, stealing her breath and clouding her vision. Her body sank to the bottom, but instead of pushing up, she stayed there. Where it was safe. But for how long? Her lungs were already screaming for oxygen. She hadn't been able to take a full breath before diving under the water. The drone's buzzing was muffled, but Megan could still hear it.

Hunting for her.

Silt drifted as she turned toward the dock. Bubbles escaped her lips as she released what little precious oxygen she had left. Kicking her feet, Megan swam closer to shore. The deepening darkness was the only indicator she had that she was in the right position. With a silent prayer, her lungs desperate for air, she surfaced.

The top of her head hit wood as she sucked in a breath with a gasp. Water lapped at the pillars holding up the dock. Megan clung to one, shivering, struggling to keep herself afloat even as her clothes dragged her back down. Her breaths were shallow. Water dripped from her hair into her eyes, clouding her vision. But the ever-present hum of the drone was there. Fear struck her hard. Now that she wasn't an option, would it go after Jax? Her grandparents? Would it burn everything on her property to the ground?

Gunshots erupted. Megan flinched, startled by the sound. The drone wavered, spinning out of control, before plummeting into the lake with a splash.

Footsteps pounded on the dock above her. "Megan!" Jax's tone was sharp, barely controlled.

He called her name again, more urgent this time.

"I'm here," she croaked, her voice weak and barely audible. She trembled violently in the water. Her feet were numb, and it was hard to feel her legs. Still, she willed herself to move away from the dock's protection to the ladder dangling in the water. Every motion felt like swimming through wet cement. Her teeth chattered. "I'm here."

Jax leaned over the edge. Stark relief flashed across his features, quickly replaced by fresh urgency. He extended his hand. "I'll pull you up."

Megan wanted to argue that he couldn't lift her out of the water, but was shivering too hard to speak. Jax was closer than the ladder. And she was so tired. Her muscles felt as weak as a newborn kitten. She reached for him, sliding her icy fingers against his warm palm.

He clamped down on her hand, his hold strong yet careful. Jax dragged her closer, then slid his other hand under her armpit. With effortless strength, as though she weighed nothing, he plucked her from the frigid water. Her teeth chattered harder as a breeze swept across her wet clothes. Her eyes drifted shut.

"No, you don't. Stay awake, Megan." Jax's tone was firm, allowing no argument. Before she could even register what was happening, he swept her into his arms, holding her close to his chest. He said something else, maybe to someone nearby, but she couldn't make out the words. Her mind felt fuzzy and slow.

She clung to his shoulders as he jogged toward the house, the heat emanating from his body a welcome contrast to her icy skin. His scent surrounded her. It was grounding. Safe.

Megan buried her face in the crook of his neck, warming her nose and lips on his bare skin. The rough prickles of his chin scraped against her temple. If she could have crawled inside of him, she would have.

He'd saved her life. Again.

Tomorrow, or maybe even later tonight, she'd be ashamed of her behavior. Embarrassed by the unabashed way she plastered herself against him. But for now, all she could think about was the warmth his body offered and the protection he provided.

For the moment, she was safe.

Megan knew, even in her half-frozen state with her mind not fully operable, that this feeling wouldn't last. She was being hunted by a killer who wouldn't stop until she was dead.

And next time, he might succeed.

ELEVEN

Megan trembled in his arms.

Jax hurried across the grass. The boathouse groaned as it listed sharply, the wooden structure surrendering to the flames. Smoke and ash filled the air. The acrid burn stung his lungs, but he ignored the ache and increased his stride toward the house. Megan couldn't stop shaking. If she didn't get warm, she would succumb to hypothermia.

The back door swung open the moment Jax's foot hit the bottom porch step. Clay ushered them inside, tossing a blanket over Megan before pointing toward the rear of the house. "Rose is already running a hot bath. I'll make tea. An ambulance is on the way."

"No... ambulance." Megan's teeth chattered violently, a clear sign her body was still in the early stages of hypothermia. She clung to Jax's shoulders. Her complexion was ghostly pale, her hair wet and limp around the delicate curves of her face.

A wave of tenderness swept over Jax. He hurried to

the bathroom attached to the primary bedroom. Rose was perched on the edge of a large bathtub, fiddling with the knobs that controlled the water temperature. Her face was pinched with worry as Jax set Megan down on the chair next to the vanity. Water dripped from her clothes onto the tile floor.

"We're going to get you warmed up fast."

He grabbed a towel from the counter and gently dried Megan's face before wrapping up her wet hair in it. Then he removed her soaked shoes and peeled off her dripping socks. Her toes were a purplish blue and frigid to the touch. Jax grabbed another towel and started rubbing them to restore circulation. Megan's whole body trembled. She clung to the blanket. "So cccold... ccccan't believe... people ddddo this for fun."

"Which part?" Jax smiled at her as he kept rubbing her feet. "Running from a fire-spewing drone or taking an impromptu dip in a freezing lake?"

"Ssswimming."

"Ah, you mean the winter swimmers. I have an uncle who loves it." Jax kept talking, hoping that it would distract her. "Uncle Jerry lives in Denmark. He swims every morning, no matter how cold it is. But he gets into a sauna afterward, so I think that makes a difference. I never tried it myself to know for sure though."

The bathroom was warming up fast, thanks to the steam coming from the bathtub. Jax dried Megan's calves and rubbed them as well to stimulate circulation. "Thank goodness you hid under the dock. I was terrified I'd have to jump in after you." He winked at her. "I'm not a fan of cold water."

She let out a weak laugh, but then her expression sobered. "You sssaved me."

"Naw. You saved yourself." Jax didn't want to think about those harrowing moments watching the fire-spewing drone chase Megan. He'd felt helpless. The decision to dive into the lake had been a brilliant one and had likely spared her life, giving Jax enough time to shoot the drone down.

He continued to rub her chilled skin. "I just pulled you from the lake and warmed your toes."

His gaze met hers and held. Jax's breath caught as something passed between them. Intangible, but powerful. He suddenly noticed the contrast of her bare skin against his. The fragile and feminine bones of her feet, the dark-pink polish on her toes, the smoothness of her skin. She was delicate, but also strong. A survivor. A fighter. And she thought of others before herself. When the drone chased her, Megan could've bolted for the house. For safety. But doing so would've put her grandparents at risk. So she'd run in the opposite direction. That said a lot about her.

"I can take it from here, Jax." Rose laid a hand on his shoulder, interrupting his train of thought.

"Right." Jax released Megan's foot and rose. She needed to get into the warm bath as soon as possible to heat her core body temperature.

As he turned away, Megan grabbed his hand. Her fingers were still icy. "Thank you, Jax."

Her voice wavered and tears shimmered in the depths of her deep brown eyes. She was terrified. For good reason. He had the indescribable urge to pull her into his arms again and hold her until all her fears were silenced, but he pushed the notion away. Instead, he gently squeezed her hand. "We'll figure out who this is, Megan, and we'll stop him. I promise."

With a nod toward Rose, Jax left the bathroom, shutting the door behind him. He wasted no time going back outside to the yard. Sirens wailed as fire trucks arrived. The wintry air was thick with a hazy smoke as the boathouse continued to burn. Everything in it would be destroyed. The mannequin—and any evidence on it—would be reduced to a pile of smoldering ashes by the time it was done. Tucker was doing his best to maintain some semblance of control, but firefighters traipsed through the crime scene willy-nilly.

Dawson exited the woods at a brisk jog. Sweat cut through the lines of soot on his face and his clothes were grass-stained from tumbling through the yard to escape the drone.

"Attacker's gone." He slid to a stop in front of Jax, panting. "There's a bend about half a mile up from the boathouse on the lake. He must've planted the mannequin and then stayed nearby, keeping watch for Megan."

Jax nodded. The mannequin had been left to draw her out to the boathouse. Chances were, the perpetrator had used the drone to monitor the property. It would've been invisible from the ground if flown at the right altitude.

Dawson bared his teeth. "I should've spotted him."

Jax shook his head. "Tucker and I were both here, and neither of us considered the attacker could be waiting nearby either. The property was cleared, and it was reasonable to believe the assailant had left. No one could've predicted he would strap a flamethrower to a drone."

A mistake Jax wouldn't make again.

The wind changed direction and smoke billowed toward them. Jax moved several paces out of the way as firefighters tugged thick hoses across the grass. An ambulance arrived. The paramedics headed into the house. Megan was probably fine, but a medical check-up was necessary.

Dawson scraped a hand through his wind-blown hair, causing it to stand in spikes. He'd lost his cowboy hat during the altercation with the drone. "Any word on your brother?"

"No." Jax's gaze swung to meet his colleague's. "Wesley didn't do this."

Sympathy creased Dawson's features. "He has a drone license—"

"I know." Frustration tightened around Jax's chest like a vise. "It looks bad. Leaving the mannequin as a diversion to draw Megan to the boathouse, arming the drone, the expert way the pilot flew it... all of it resembles military tactics. But again, my brother is a Navy SEAL. Why go to all this trouble when he could just slip up behind Megan in the dark and slit her throat? Someone is framing Wesley, and I don't know why."

Dawson didn't reply. What could he say? Jax wasn't a fool. He knew how he sounded. Like a brother in denial. It struck him then—he'd been horribly wrong about Megan. He hadn't seen things clearly. Was he doing the same now? It was an awful thought. Jax didn't want to believe for a second that Wesley would commit murder. Yes, he was a soldier. Yes, he'd been to war. But operating outside the bounds of the law was a very different matter.

"Megan told me of a guy named Zeke Russell," Jax continued. "He was Oliver's drug dealer, and it sounds like he was a part of an illegal fighting ring. My brother believed someone was trying to kill him. Maybe it was Zeke."

Dawson ripped off his hoodie and used the shirt beneath it to wipe the sweat and soot from his face. "Does Zeke know Wesley? What reason would he have for framing your brother for this?"

"I don't know. Wesley and Oliver were twins. They ran in the same circles until Oliver started using, but even then, they were close. According to Megan, Zeke got violent with Oliver. If Wesley found out..." Jax blew out a breath. "I could see him confronting Zeke about it."

Dawson grunted and dropped the shirt from his face. "What else can you tell me about him?"

"Not much. He and his brother, Cody, own a gym called Bodybuilders. Megan may know more, but she's not in a position to be questioned." Jax's gaze flicked to the flaming boathouse and the firemen working hard to contain the fire. "If Megan's right and Zeke was running some kind of illegal fighting ring, any number of people could've wanted Oliver dead. We can't assume Zeke is behind this, but he may have insight into who might be. Either way, we should find him."

"Agreed."

Jax breathed out a sigh of relief. "Thanks."

Dawson's gaze shifted from the burning boathouse and focused on Jax. The steel in his tone belied the sympathy in his eyes. "Don't thank me yet. We've always been honest with each other, so I'm gonna be straight with you now. I have serious doubts about your assertion that Wesley is being framed. There's not a shred of evidence to support the theory."

Jax couldn't argue with Dawson's logic, so he didn't even try. "Someone wants Megan dead. That much is a fact. We have to follow all leads until we have direct evidence that points to a clear suspect. One photograph isn't enough to say Wesley is guilty of this."

"No, but it indicates a personal connection to your family. If we find solid evidence proving Wesley is behind this, he'll be arrested and charged. We all care about you, Jax, but we won't ignore our duty."

"I'd never ask you to."

Dawson sighed. "I know, but it'll feel like a betrayal all the same."

TWELVE

"I'm scared."

Megan's voice trembled as she clutched the phone to her ear. She was buried under a thick blanket on the couch, her knees tucked underneath her. Her father's Bible rested on her lap. It'd been hours since the attack, but the tension in her muscles refused to ease.

The house was still and quiet. Her grandparents had gone to bed an hour ago. Exhaustion dragged at Megan's body, but every time she closed her eyes, her mind betrayed her. All she could see was the drone, its flames streaking through the air, and the myriad ways the nightmare could've ended differently.

Unsettled and in desperate need of a lifeline, she'd called her sponsor Sandy McMillian. Thirty years sober and the definition of tough love, Sandy was the type of person who told you what you needed to hear, not what you wanted. Back when Megan lived in Fort Worth, they'd often meet for coffee or sit side by side at NA meetings, but even now, miles apart, Sandy was always just a phone call away.

"Grateful doesn't begin to cover it," Megan whispered, tracing her fingers along the worn leather cover of her father's Bible. "No one was seriously hurt today, and that's a miracle. But it feels like my life is spinning out of control, Sandy. I don't know how far this person will go to kill me. What if..." Her voice cracked, and she took a shaky breath. "What if the next time someone gets seriously hurt?"

The silence on the other end of the line stretched just long enough for Megan to realize how tightly she gripped the phone.

Sandy sighed. "You're scared, and you have every right to be, hon. What happened today was terrifying. But fear doesn't get to drive the bus. You hear me? It's a passenger. Let it sit there, sure—but you keep your hands on the wheel."

"I know, but..." Megan's thumb brushed over the gilded edges of the Bible. "It's hard to block out the fear and worry, no matter how much I pray or try to focus on the positive. God's in control, I know that, but..."

She didn't know how to put into words everything she was feeling. It was all muddled together. All Megan knew was the last time she'd felt like this was when her mom died. Then again, after Oliver's accident. Both times, she'd run away from her problems. The first time by using drugs, the second by leaving town. The instinct to run away again pulsed through her veins like a battle cry. It was difficult to hold it back.

"I want to face this head-on, but I'm not sure I have the strength to do it." Megan finally found the words for her deepest fears. "What if I discover all this hard work I've done to better myself has been for nothing?"

"I don't believe that for a second." Sandy's words were immediate and full of conviction. "You're stronger than you know. And you're not doing this alone. You've got your grandparents, your friends, and your coworkers. You've got that detective you mentioned. What's his name? Jax? You've got me. But most importantly, you've got God. Lean on your support system. That's what we're here for."

Sandy was right. In the past, Megan had shied away from asking for help. She'd been too prideful, too independent. Recovery had taught her that when struggles came, relying on others was essential.

She drew in a deep breath. "I don't need to have all the answers."

"No, you don't. Focus on what you can control, and do the next right thing." The older woman's voice softened. "When life feels overwhelming, take it moment by moment. Breathe, pray, and remember, you aren't fighting this battle alone."

"Thank you, Sandy. I needed to hear that." Megan drew in another deep breath and felt the tight knot of fear in her stomach loosen. "I'm sorry for calling so late. Thanks for talking with me."

"You can call anytime, honey. I'm always here. And I know things are up in the air, but go to a meeting if you can. It'll help ground you."

"I will." Megan was supposed to lead the NA meeting tomorrow night, but after the drone attack, she'd asked Douglas to fill in for her. She didn't want to risk anyone else getting caught in the crossfire. But as soon as it was safe, she would go to a meeting. "Goodnight, Sandy."

She hung up and let the stillness of the house seep into her. The blinds overlooking the backyard were tilted open, the outline of the charred boathouse visible in the faint moonlight. Nestled under the warm blanket, sleep beckoned. She was safe. Chief Garcia had posted a patrol officer at the front of the house to stand guard for the night. Nothing bad would happen.

Megan leaned her head back against the sofa cushion and yawned.

A shadow shifted in the yard.

She jolted into a sitting position, her heart taking off like a runaway jackrabbit. The blanket fell from her body, letting the cold air rush in. Goosebumps pricked her skin. She rose from the couch to peer through the blinds. Someone was in the yard. A man. Strolling past the boathouse toward the back door.

A scream lodged in Megan's throat, and then a sliver of moonlight cut across the intruder's face.

Jax.

She pressed a hand to her chest as if that would slow her racing pulse and dragged in a deep breath before whirling on her heel. Frigid air washed over her bare arms when she opened the back door. The porch boards were icy even through her thick socks. "Jax, what on earth are you doing here? You nearly gave me a heart attack."

He emerged from the darkness, the harsh porch light casting a long shadow behind him. "I'm keeping watch. Sorry if I scared you." Jax made a shooing motion with his hands, indicating Megan should go back inside. He followed behind her, locking the door and then securing the alarm. Only then did he turn back to face her. "I thought you were asleep."

"Clearly not." The words came out harsher than she intended, but her heart was still racing. She forced her tone back into neutral territory. "Chief Garcia posted an officer in the driveway. Isn't Tucker still there?"

"Yes, but if there's an emergency, he'll be called away to handle it, leaving you unprotected. I didn't want to take the risk."

The last of Megan's temper cooled. Jax was going above and beyond, and she'd been harsh with him. "I'm sorry for being short. Thank you for keeping an eye on us."

"It's nothing." He shrugged.

But it wasn't nothing. The overhead kitchen light was off, but the under-cabinet LEDs cast enough of a glow for Megan to see Jax's bedraggled appearance. Whiskers coated his jaw and cheeks. Weariness drew faint lines at the corners of his eyes and the tip of his nose was red from the cold. Her heart softened even more, and she gestured to a kitchen chair. "Sit. I'll make you some coffee."

"That's unnecessary—"

"Sit, Jax." She gently pushed him toward a chair. "Don't make me wake up Nana."

He chuckled and collapsed into the closest seat. "Your grandmother is a powerhouse."

Earlier in the evening, Nana had plied every one of the police officers and firefighters with coffee and food. Perpetually in motion, with a warm smile for everyone, she'd refused to take no for an answer.

Megan smiled. "Everyone thinks Pops is the toughest in our family, but he doesn't hold a candle to Nana. She has a way of convincing you to do her bidding without you even realizing it."

Megan started coffee brewing and then noticed a pot of homemade hot chocolate on the stove. Nana had made it for the first responders. Megan touched the metal and discovered the pot was still warm. Turning on the burner, she used a whisk to keep the sweet drink from burning while it heated.

Jax's gaze followed her every move. It was strange to have him in her kitchen, the house around them silent. Megan was suddenly very aware that she was dressed in pajama pants and a T-shirt. The clothing was modest, but also intimate. The memory of the way he'd plucked her from the lake and the feel of his arms holding her close rose, unbidden, in her mind. Heat climbed into her cheeks.

Embarrassed, she hid her face behind a curtain of hair. Jax was a law enforcement officer, and while he was undoubtedly courageous, it was his job to protect the citizens of Knoxville. He would have put himself in the line of fire for anyone. She wasn't special, and it would be very dangerous to allow this spark of attraction to grow. They may have found an uneasy peace this afternoon, but Oliver's death was an integral part of their history and always would be. There was no way to move past it.

Megan poured the hot chocolate into a mug and then some coffee for Jax. "Would you like cream? Or sugar?"

"Black is fine."

She handed him the mug, careful not to let their fingers brush, and then claimed the chair across from him. The warm scents of chocolate and nutmeg filled the air as she sipped her hot cocoa. The warmth settled in her belly and fortified her for the conversation to come. "I'd like to know what the stalker left for me at the boathouse. Chief Garcia took my statement and asked questions, but before I could find out what kicked all this off, he was pulled away."

Jax hesitated and then pulled out his phone. He opened the photo app. "Before I show you this, remember, it's not real. It's a mannequin."

She nodded, sucking in a breath to brace herself.

He turned the phone to face her, and the crime scene photo came into view. Shock froze her muscles. The mannequin was shockingly lifelike, the blood coating its neck and clothing gruesome. Nothing could have prepared her for this. "She looks like me."

A tremble rippled through her. This wasn't just a decoy, designed to pull her out to the boathouse, so she was vulnerable to an attack from the drone. The mannequin was meant to scare her. Just like the emails.

Megan didn't specialize in criminology, but she'd taken some courses on the subject during college. "He wants me to be afraid. It's not enough to kill me. He wants to terrorize me." She breathed out. "This isn't just about getting revenge for Oliver's death. This is personal. Whoever is behind this hates me."

Jax pulled his phone away and clicked it off. Then he reached across the table and touched her hand. "He won't get to you. I promise. But we need to discuss the steps necessary to keep you safe."

"I've already canceled my appointments for tomorrow." Megan hated letting her clients down, but she wouldn't risk putting them in harm's way. The drone had shot at the boathouse, nearly killing Jax and Dawson in the process. This was bigger than her. She needed to play it smart. "I'll try to stay home as much as possible. Of course, I can't do that forever, but I told Chief Garcia everything I know about Zeke Russell. Hopefully, something will break in the case and this will all be over soon."

Megan didn't want Zeke to be behind this. She'd never liked the man, but it'd been ten years since she'd last seen him. People changed. God knew she had. Zeke could have turned his life around, and a part of her prayed that was the case. Then again, it wasn't any better if Wesley was responsible for these attacks.

"The investigation may take time." Jax's tone was gentle. "I don't want to scare you, but it would be smart to take additional measures. The police department is short-staffed, and while I know Chief Garcia will do all he can, a patrol officer can't be stationed here 24-7. Based on the attacks, this perpetrator is smart and determined. I'd like for you to consider having the Special Forces guard the property and your grandparents."

The Special Forces was a nickname given to a group of retired veterans who lived in Knoxville. Megan knew many of them and was friendly with their wives. In fact, the ladies had all texted or called to check in when word broke that Megan had been attacked. She was touched they'd be willing to protect her, but every member of the Special Forces was married now with a family.

"Do you really think it's necessary?"

"I do. In fact, Tucker's already been organizing the shifts." Jax tilted his head. "I didn't know you helped Tucker and Leah with Kaylee Ross's disappearance."

Megan shrugged. "I answered some questions, that's all." She'd been just as worried as Leah about Kaylee's disappearance and was glad the case resolved happily. "No one owes me any favors for doing the right thing."

"I don't think they see it as repaying a favor. They want to help, and I think it'll make everyone feel more secure to know the house and your grandparents are protected."

She breathed out. He was right. It would make her feel a lot better. "Okay then. Thank you."

"Good, that takes care of the house and your grandparents, but there's still you. As you said, you can't stay in your house forever. In the meantime, I've discussed the matter with Chief Garcia, and unless you object, he's agreed to give me temporary leave from my duties so I can stay close to you."

She blinked. Tonight had been one surprise after another, but this one might be the biggest of all. "But... what about the investigation?"

"It's better for everyone if I'm not involved." Jax drew in a deep breath and let it out slowly. "My brother is considered a person of interest in these attacks on you. I think Wesley is being framed, but what if he isn't? Noah, Dawson, and Chief Garcia have to follow the evidence wherever it leads without worrying about how I'll handle it. I need to put my faith in my team. And God. Right now, the best way I can help is by keeping you safe."

Megan hesitated. "Jax... are you sure? I didn't cause the accident that killed Oliver, but I was still driving the car. I'm still a part of it. No one would blame you for putting some distance between us, including me."

He met her gaze. Held it. Buried in those dark blue orbs was a warmth that sucker punched her right in the stomach.

"I appreciate that, Megan. More than you know. But I need to do this. By keeping you safe, I give Chief Garcia, Noah, and the rest of the team the ability to focus on finding the man behind this. It's possible the person responsible for these attacks on you is seeking vigilante justice, but my heart and my gut say it's a lot deeper than that. I believe whoever killed Oliver is after you now. The quicker Chief Garcia finds him, the safer everyone will be."

Jax's gaze dropped to his coffee. "And the sooner my family will have the answers—and the justice—they need to put this all behind us."

THIRTEEN

An icy breeze slid down the collar of Jax's coat as he paced the shoreline between Megan's house and the lake. Police boats bobbed on the water, their lights casting faint ripples against the surface. Divers in black suits pitched themselves off the larger vessel, disappearing into the still, murky depths. They were searching for the drone Jax had shot down yesterday. It wouldn't be an easy recovery. The lake was deep, its bottom tangled with weeds and silt, but finding the device was critical. It could hold the key to identifying the perpetrator.

Jax's phone buzzed in his pocket. He pulled it out, glanced at the screen, and his stomach tightened. Swiping to answer, he said, "Hi, Mom. Have you heard anything about Wesley?"

"Nothing yet. Your dad drove to Ridgewood this afternoon. One of Wesley's old buddies started some kind of private investigation firm last year. He's hoping they might help."

Jax pressed his thumb and forefinger to the bridge of his nose. Filing a missing person's report had crossed his mind more than once, but it was a last resort. Law enforcement already had their hands full, and there wasn't proof that Wesley was in any real danger. Not yet, anyway. But if his brother stayed off the grid for a few more days, that might change. Wesley had never disappeared for more than a week before.

"*Mijo*, I should warn you," his mother said, her voice hesitant. Jax could picture her chewing her lip nervously, the way she always did when delivering bad news. "Your dad heard rumors this morning. He thinks you're acting as Megan Ingles's bodyguard. He nearly drove over to the house to confront you about it, but I convinced him finding Wesley was more important."

The pounding in Jax's head intensified. Dropping his hand from his face, he let the wind coming off the lake cool his skin. This wasn't how he wanted to have this conversation with his parents. He'd planned to explain things in person, but with everything happening so fast, there hadn't been time.

"Someone is trying to kill her," Jax said, his tone low but firm. "I think it's connected to the night Oliver died. It's a long, complicated story, and I can't tell you much since it's an active investigation, but I need you and Dad to trust me. I'm trying to do the right thing."

He turned to glance back at Megan's house. He'd left her in the kitchen, baking cookies with her grandmother, gospel music softly playing on the radio. Spending the day with the Ingles family—with Megan—had revealed a lot. They were warm and funny. It had reinforced what he'd already realized: he'd made a terrible mistake. Prayer and careful reflection had shifted his perspective. Megan hadn't deserved the blame they'd heaped on her. She certainly didn't deserve to be stalked and nearly killed by a madman.

The trouble was, Jax still didn't have solid proof of her innocence. He could only hope the investigation would uncover enough evidence to convince his family— and himself—that she wasn't responsible for Oliver's death.

"I promise to explain everything when I can," Jax said, shifting his attention back to the conversation with his mother.

"*Mi amor...*" Her voice wavered, and for a moment, Jax could hear her struggling to find the right words. Then she prayed in Spanish. She asked for wisdom and guidance, her words steady and reverent. Jax's heart twisted. Oliver's death had changed his mother forever. Now, with Wesley missing and Jax protecting Megan, he knew she was carrying a heavy burden of worry.

When her prayer ended, Valentina sighed. "Of course you should do what you believe is right. I raised you to be independent and strong. I can't be angry with you for following your convictions, even if I don't under- stand them. When your dad comes back, I'll explain to him what we've discussed. I can't promise he'll see it my way. He's his own person. But I'll try to convince him not to rush to judgment."

If anyone could get through to his dad, it was his

mother. Jax wanted to reach through the phone and give her a hug. "Thanks, Mamacita. I love you."

"I love you too, *mijo*. Stay safe."

As Jax hung up, a branch snapped behind him. He turned, half-expecting it to be Jason Gonzalez. The former Marine was a member of the Special Forces. Jason, along with Nathan Hollister, had taken the first shift guarding the Ingles property. But to his surprise, it was Megan's grandfather. Clay hadn't said more than five words to Jax all day. It was strange that he'd sought him out now. Then again, maybe it was time the two men hashed out their differences.

Jax nodded in greeting and then turned back to check on the divers. It didn't appear they'd found the drone yet, judging from the way everyone was peering overboard.

Clay joined him. "You screwed up yesterday. I told you it wasn't a good idea for Megan to go out to the boathouse and you ignored me. She's strong, but everyone has a breaking point. The mannequin... she didn't need to see that. And by taking her outside, you put her in harm's way."

"You're right. I made a bad call. No one could've expected Megan would be attacked by a drone with a flamethrower attached, but..." Guilt gnawed at him. "That doesn't matter. She was almost killed. I take responsibility for that."

"And what about everything else?" Clay's tone was bitter. "The accusations you've leveled against her have caused more pain than you can imagine. My granddaughter has made her fair share of mistakes, I won't deny that, but to be called a murderer?" He shook his head. "Megan was stone-cold sober when the accident happened. The survivors' guilt, town gossip, and constant judgment drove her away. Leaving was the right decision, for her and for her sobriety, but it was hard on Rose and me. We missed having her near. Coming back to Knoxville wasn't easy for Megan, but when Rose got cancer..."

He paused, seemingly overcome with emotion, before he cleared his throat and continued, "When Rose got cancer, Megan didn't hesitate to move back. She helped us get through a difficult time, and I'm so proud of the woman she's become." Clay turned to face Jax, his expression hard and unyielding. "I won't have you, or anyone else, threatening to destroy the life she's built for herself."

Jax felt the heat of the older man's anger, but it didn't spark his own. Clay was protecting Megan. That was his job as her grandfather, and it was a position Jax respected. He wasn't sure there were any words he could offer that would calm Clay's ire. But maybe that wasn't the point.

He drew in a breath and let it out slowly. "You're angry and you have every right to be, but don't let that cloud your judgment. Megan's life is in danger and she needs protection. I can provide it." Jax met Clay's glare. "I don't know who is after her, or how it's connected to Oliver's death, but it's my intention to get to the truth. That's all I've ever wanted."

Clay was quiet for a long moment, assessing him.

Then he turned to face the lake again. "I know what it's like to feel a grief so deep it turns you inside out. Rose and I buried our only child, Robert, nearly thirty years ago, but there are some days, it feels like he just passed. Megan is all we have left. I'm protective. But I'm wise enough to realize we aren't the only ones hurting." He tucked his wrinkled hands into the pockets of his corduroy jacket. "I'm sorry about Oliver. I hope you find the answers you're looking for."

The unexpected kindness caused a swell of emotion in Jax. Tears burned his eyes, catching him off guard. He blinked them back. "Thank you, sir."

Clay turned and headed for the house. The conversation hadn't solved things, but it'd brokered a temporary peace. That was enough.

Jax stood on the shore, watching the dive team, until his rolling emotions settled. Dark clouds hovered in the distance. An arctic front was headed their way. It would drop the temperatures below freezing. There might even be snow, a rare occurrence for this part of Texas.

All the more reason it was important to find the drone today.

Jason Gonzalez strolled down the side yard along the tree line. Scars crisscrossed the former Marine's left cheek, remnants of an IED explosion that had killed the rest of his unit. At his side was his trusted German shepherd, Connor. The dog had a beautiful black and brown coat, but like his master, scars cut along his left side. Connor was also former military, a retired bomb detection dog.

"Everything okay?" Jax asked as they drew closer.

"No signs of trouble." Jason adjusted the ski cap covering his dark hair until it protected the tops of his ears. "Nathan is monitoring the front part of the property. We'll switch shifts in an hour with Walker and Logan."

Nathan Hollister was a former Green Beret. Married with a daughter, he owned a ranch that also operated as a horse rescue. Walker Montgomery also owned a ranch and his wife, Hayley, worked at the police department. Logan Keller was a paramedic. The former Army medic had been on duty last night and had given Megan an exam to make sure she wasn't suffering from any lingering effects of hypothermia after her dip in the lake.

"Can't tell you how much I appreciate y'all being here." Jax scratched Connor behind the ears. The dog's tongue lolled out in happiness.

"No need to thank us. We're happy to do it." Jason's gaze went to the police boats out on the water. "No one should be hunted down and threatened." His gaze swung back to Jax. "You should know, I've tried reaching out to your brother several times since he's come home. Wesley wasn't interested in joining our informal support group. For some guys, even among fellow soldiers, opening up can be hard."

Jax sighed. "He's stubborn. And far too independent."

"That's the impression I got too. He's suffering from PTSD, but I never had the impression it was out of control. Being out in the wilderness, connecting with nature... that seemed to be his version of therapy." Jason's mouth flattened into a thin line. "It's not my place to say, and I don't have any inside information, but from a personal standpoint, I'd find it difficult to believe Wesley was behind this."

A knot of tension unfurled in Jax. It was nice to hear that someone outside of the situation had the same assessment of Wesley. "Thank you for saying that."

The sound of a vehicle turning in the driveway caught Jax's attention. It was a Knoxville Police Department SUV. Noah and Dawson emerged. Jax lifted his hand in a wave as he jogged across the yard to meet them. "They haven't found the drone yet. Still looking."

"We aren't here about that." Noah looked weary, deep lines bracketing his mouth. "It's Zeke Russell. Where's Megan?"

Dread curled inside Jax. He didn't like the look on Noah's face. Whatever his colleague had come to say, it wasn't good. "She's inside." Jax's gaze darted to Dawson, who also wore a grim expression. "What's going on?"

"It's better if we speak to you together," Noah answered. "I have some follow-up questions anyway."

Worry fueling his steps, Jax led them into the house. The scent of vanilla and butter hung heavy in the air. Chatter and music spilled from the kitchen. He pointed to the living room and said, "I'll get Megan." Jax's strides were long as he crossed the dining room, even as his mind whirled with possibilities.

He rounded the corner and stopped short. Megan

stood at the island in the center. A caramel-colored sweater highlighted the reddish tones in her blonde hair and clung to her slender form. Mid-laugh, her eyes sparkled with humor and her cheeks were flushed with the heat from the oven. And when she noticed him in the doorway, her smile widened.

Jax stared at her, mesmerized. Had he ever seen her like this? Happy and carefree? Their previous interactions had always been so fraught with tension, and since the attacks, worry had entrenched itself in her features. So no, he didn't think he'd ever seen her like this.

It stole his breath.

Megan was an objectively beautiful woman, but happiness enhanced her beauty, making her radiant. His pulse skipped a beat. Unsettled by his reaction, he tried to tell her that Noah and Dawson were here, but the words died on his lips. Jax couldn't quite bring himself to ruin the happy moment she'd found. Not after everything she'd been through the last few days.

"Jax!" Megan used a spatula to lift a cookie from a baking tray. "Perfect timing. Settle a debate between Nana and I. Should walnuts be included in chocolate chip cookies or not?"

Rose smiled from her station at the mixing bowl. Her eyebrows drew down into a mock scowl, but a smile played on her lips. "May I remind you, I'm the expert in the room. Walnuts do *not* belong in chocolate chip cookies. I'm sure Jax will agree with me."

He held up his hands in mock surrender. It seemed

dangerous to step into this debate. "Walnuts or no walnuts, if it's a chocolate chip cookie, count me in. Actually, any cookie will do." He winked at Megan. "Although I do like nuts."

"Ha!" She pointed her spatula at her grandmother. "I told you!"

Nana maturely stuck out her tongue, which made Jax laugh. Knowing that Noah and Dawson were waiting in the other room should've been at the forefront of his mind, but it was nice to disappear into the joyful kitchen and forget about the problems plaguing them for a minute or two more.

Jax scanned the cookies covering the counter. "It looks like you're baking for an army."

"It's for the Special Forces. We'll send some home with Jason and Nathan when they leave." Megan scooped another cookie off the tray. "We also baked extra for the police department. It doesn't come close to thanking them for everything they're doing, but I wanted to let them know how much I appreciate their hard work."

It was a sweet and unnecessary gesture, but it summed up everything Jax was learning about Megan. She was considerate and unfailingly kind. How could he have ever thought she'd killed his brother and then tried to avoid responsibility for it? Noah had been right. It wasn't in her nature. In the past, drugs might've made her a different person, one he wouldn't recognize, but this Megan... she wasn't capable of what he'd accused her of.

It made what he had to say next all that much harder.

Jax drew in a breath. "Megan, I'm sorry, but Noah and Dawson are here. They're waiting in the living room to speak to us about Zeke. I don't think they've found him yet, and they need to ask some more questions."

It was painful to see the happiness melt from her pretty features, replaced by worry and concern. The flush in her cheeks faded and her mouth flattened. "Nana, can you make a fresh pot of coffee? I'm sure Noah and Dawson would like some."

With deliberate movements, she untied her apron and slipped it off before squaring her shoulders. Jax admired the way she shifted into battle mode. None of this was easy. He was a police officer with decades of experience, and even his emotions were riding a roller coaster. He couldn't imagine what it must be like for her.

How much more could Megan take before breaking? Jax didn't know, and it added a fresh worry to his growing pile. These threats on her life, the pressure she was under... he didn't want it to drive her back into bad decisions. Megan had been sober for a long time, but even she'd admitted in the hospital that it was a daily choice.

If she was pushed hard enough, would she return to drugs? The thought terrified him.

He cared about her. More than he wanted to admit, and it added another layer to their already complicated relationship. Protecting Megan from a killer was his duty. Finding the man who'd murdered Oliver would provide closure for his family. Forming a relationship—even a friendship—with the woman who'd been driving the car when his brother was killed... that was a step too far.

His family would never accept it. And if Jax needed to remind himself of it daily, then he would. Once this case was over, he and Megan would go their separate ways. There would be peace between them, but nothing else.

Absolutely nothing else.

FOURTEEN

"Sorry to drop in without calling first." Noah took a sip of his coffee before setting it down on a coaster.

He'd claimed her grandfather's recliner. Dawson had opted to stand next to the fireplace while Jax and Megan were on the sofa. Jax sat close enough that his shoulder brushed against hers, and without thinking, she leaned into him. His solid presence soothed the nerves jittering her insides. Talking about the threats against her, even thinking about them, was difficult. It dragged up memories of the night Oliver died. The terror of being run off the road, the sound of metal crashing against metal, the pain exploding in her body.

Focus on the next right thing.

Megan drew in a breath, pushing away the memories that threatened to drown her. Doing whatever she could to help the police was the next right thing.

"We have an update, but first, I need to ask a few questions." Noah opened his tablet and removed the electronic pen. "Megan, when was the last time you saw or spoke to Zeke Russell?"

She considered his question. "I don't remember the exact date, but it was before I went to rehab. After I got clean, I cut everyone associated with that part of my life off."

"You mentioned Zeke sold drugs to Oliver. What about others?"

"I assume so." Megan clasped her hands together in her lap. Her fingers were icy, despite the warm temperature of the house. "I never bought from him though. Zeke always scared me. Even before I saw him become violent with Oliver. It's hard to explain... it was more of a feeling. Like I knew once he got me under his thumb, I'd never get out."

Survival was a funny thing. Back then, Megan hadn't had any qualms about taking drugs, stealing, or heaven help her, even driving while under the influence. And yet, she'd drawn the line at buying drugs from Zeke. Why? She couldn't explain it. The only reasonable explanation was that she hadn't been completely suicidal. Just reckless and incredibly stupid.

Noah leaned forward, planting his elbows on his knees. "Who else bought drugs from Zeke?"

Megan hesitated. "I can give you the names of people who hung out with Oliver and me back then, but I haven't been in contact with most of them for ten years. The few people I still speak to are sober now. None of them live in Knoxville anymore. I don't want to disrupt their lives and stir up bad memories if it's not necessary."

Her gaze skipped to Dawson, whose expression was impassive, before settling back on Noah. "Why are you asking these questions? Weren't you able to find Zeke?"

"Not exactly." Dawson frowned. He removed his cowboy hat and tossed it on the cushion of an armchair before running his hands through his hair. "We ran him through our databases. He has a 2014 Ford Explorer in his name and a current driver's license. The address listed on both is a house on the outskirts of town owned by his mother. She confirmed Zeke lives there, but he comes and goes. She hasn't seen him for days. Not since he came to pick up his disability check last week."

"Disability check?" Jax straightened. "Is he on Social Security disability?"

"Nope. He's receiving disability from the VA for injuries sustained while on deployment." He gave Jax a pointed look. "Zeke was a Night Stalker."

Megan had never heard the term before. "What's a Night Stalker?"

"It's a special ops unit in the Army, specifically the 160th Special Operations Aviation Regiment," Jax said. "They're known for being proficient in nighttime operations."

She sucked in a breath. The attacks on her had been well-planned and indicated the perpetrator had a military background. It was part of the reason Chief Garcia thought Wesley was behind them. But if Zeke also had special ops training...

Jax turned toward her. "Did you know Zeke had been in the military?"

She shook her head. "I did my best to steer clear of Zeke from the day I met him. In fact, I tried to get Oliver to stop buying drugs from him, to stop fighting for him, but he wouldn't listen." Megan's attention shifted back to Dawson and Noah. "What about the gym Zeke owned? Bodybuilders."

"It shut down a week after Oliver died. The sheriff's department raided the gym on suspicion of drug trafficking and operating an illegal fighting ring. They even issued an arrest warrant for Zeke, but the DA later retracted it, saying the case wasn't strong enough to hold up in court. We're attempting to track down any of the old employees who worked there, hoping they can provide more insight." Noah held Megan's gaze. "That's why I need the names of the other people Zeke was selling to. Maybe they know where he is now. Or who his friends are."

"His mom doesn't know?" Jax asked, his tone incredulous. "His check is delivered to her house. He pops by there to pick it up, right?"

"Yes, but his mom wasn't very forthcoming. I suspect she knows more than she's saying, but doesn't want Zeke to get in trouble. She provided us with a phone number, but Zeke's not answering. We interviewed his older brother, Cody Russell. He swears up and down that the sheriff's raid on Bodybuilders was based on false claims and both he and his brother were innocent. Cody couldn't tell us who any of his brother's friends were and doesn't know where Zeke stays when he's not at their mother's."

Jax's brows drew down in suspicion. "They're covering for him."

Dawson shrugged. "They're definitely not sharing all they know."

"Does Zeke have a criminal record?"

"Yep. He's been arrested for drug possession, assault, and domestic violence. Nothing recent though." Noah pulled some pages from a pocket on his tablet cover and handed them to Jax.

Megan leaned over to get a look. Her stomach twisted. The first page had a photograph of Zeke, taken when he was arrested for assaulting his girlfriend right before Oliver died. He looked exactly as she remembered —a bloated, meaty face with sunken eyes that spoke of sleepless nights and drug use. The arrest record listed his height as 6'0 and his weight as 240 pounds. Judging by the thickness of his neck and the way his shirtsleeves barely encircled his arms, most of that was muscle.

Her mind flashed back to the first attack, the feel of the attacker's arm trapping her against the seat. He'd been powerful. Someone who worked out.

Someone like Zeke.

Jax flipped to the last page and frowned. "Zeke's last arrest happened right before Oliver died and then... nothing for the last ten years? That's strange. He wasn't in constant trouble, but there's an arrest every few years here. I find it hard to believe he miraculously cleaned up his act."

"We thought that was weird too." Dawson bent over the coffee table, plucking a Snickerdoodle from the plate of cookies. "It's possible Zeke is lying low. Or the raid on his gym scared him and he's living under a fake identity." He bit into the cookie, eating half of it in one go. After chewing and swallowing, Dawson added, "We questioned some of the Russells' neighbors, and this is where it gets weird. None of them have seen Zeke or his truck in years."

Megan's mind whirled as she tried to figure out how to put the puzzle pieces together. "Let me see if I have this right. Zeke and his older brother, Cody, own a gym together. The sheriff's department investigates them for drug trafficking and running an illegal fighting ring. One week after Oliver dies, the gym shuts down and Zeke skips town. He receives a monthly disability check, which he collects from his mother, but neither she nor his brother claim to have any idea where he lives. He's not answering his phone, hasn't been arrested since Oliver died, and the neighbors haven't seen him in years."

Noah nodded. "That sums it up all right."

Jax rose from the couch and began pacing the room. "So let's assume Zeke, who was known to have a violent temper, got into an altercation with Oliver. In anger, he runs Oliver and Megan off the road, killing my brother. Afraid he'll be outed for murder, he goes into hiding, only to have his gym raided by the sheriff's department a week later. Zeke decides to start over somewhere else, taking on a fake identity to do it. He thinks he's free and clear, but then I reopen the investigation into Oliver's accident. Afraid that Megan may put two and two together, he attempts to silence her."

"It's a good theory." Dawson wiped his hands on a napkin. "But there are some holes. Why wait to kill Megan? You reopened the investigation into the accident weeks ago. Not to mention, if Zeke is living under a new identity, what does he care if we start digging into the past?"

Jax stopped pacing. "Because he's involved in a new criminal enterprise. The sheriff's office couldn't prove he was trafficking drugs or running an illegal fighting ring, but we know he was. Chances are, Zeke moved his operation to wherever he's living now. We find him, we may discover running Oliver off the road was only the tip of the iceberg." He turned and planted his hands on the back of the armchair. "Zeke doesn't want us looking for him. He definitely doesn't want Megan telling us what she knows about his old operation."

She pressed a hand to her midsection. Her stomach churned, and she regretted eating two cookies earlier. "I don't know that much."

"You might know more than you realize. Or Zeke's just scared. Either way, I think he's hoping to clean up a loose end."

She hated this. All of it. But even Megan couldn't deny Jax had connected the dots in a logical line that led straight to her. She swallowed down the fear threatening to rise up and met Noah's gaze. "I'll give you the names of everyone I know who bought from Zeke or was associated with him. I hope it helps."

For the next hour, she talked.

When she was finished, she slumped against the

couch cushions. Her voice was hoarse, and a headache brewed along her temples. Discussing the people she'd done drugs with and the world she'd been a part of dredged up a lot of shame and guilt. Megan wasn't that person anymore, but it was still painful to remember how she'd once been.

Noah, who'd taken notes, closed his tablet case. "Thank you, Megan. We'll follow up on all of this information and update you once we know more." He turned to Jax. "No news on Wesley?"

"No. My parents are still looking for him. As soon as we make contact, we'll have him call you."

Megan wrapped her arms around her waist. She wasn't sure what to think. Was Zeke trying to tie up a loose end, as Jax suspected? Or was Wesley out for revenge? The emails she'd received would suggest the latter, as did the photograph of Oliver and his brothers dropped at the crime scene.

Clearly, Noah was still pursuing the possibility that Wesley was responsible for the attacks.

"I'll walk you out." Jax escorted Dawson and Noah outside.

Megan eyed the dirty plates on the coffee table, but didn't have the strength to clean up yet. Instead, she leaned against the back of the couch and closed her eyes, letting the quiet settle over her. Her headache eased slightly. Still, she felt unmoored, adrift on a sea of past transgressions.

When Jax returned, she didn't move but opened her eyes. "I know there's some risk, but do you think I could go to the NA meeting tonight? I asked Douglas to run it, but it would be good for me to attend."

Jax crossed the room and sat next to her on the couch. Worry creased his features. "Are you..."

"No." She shook her head to emphasize her words. "I won't use again. Ever. But talking about my past has brought up a lot of negative feelings. Attending a meeting, being around people who understand what it's like, helps. It's a support system and a healthy coping mechanism. Kinda like attending church. That also helps, but there's no service tonight."

"What time is the NA meeting?"

"Seven. It's at the Prince of Peace." The local church in the center of town had a large conference room. "The meeting is open, so it won't be just people in recovery. It'll be friends and family too. Anyone curious about how to support a loved one in recovery is welcome. Normally, we have about 50 people."

He seemed to calculate something in his head and then nodded. "Okay. I think it'll be safe to go. I'll attend the meeting with you. A patrol unit can make rounds before and during the meeting, which will add an extra layer of protection."

It was a lot of maneuvering just to attend tonight's meeting, and Megan was momentarily tempted to tell Jax to forget it, but she snuffed out the urge. Surviving these attacks wouldn't matter if she fell apart at the seams. In times of crisis, it was important to reach out for help from her support system.

Megan picked up Zeke's arrest record from the coffee

table. His piercing glare sent a tremble of fear down her spine. It was instinctive, a visceral reaction she couldn't entirely suppress, and she hated herself for it. "A part of me hopes that when Dawson and Noah find Zeke, they learn he's turned his life around."

"People like Zeke don't change."

The cynicism in Jax's tone landed like a stone between them. Megan tilted her head, studying him. "I suppose working in law enforcement means you've seen the worst in people."

"Repeatedly," he said grimly. "Money, drugs, power, and greed are powerful motivators." He jerked his chin toward Zeke's picture. "Someone like him... he'd turn on his own mother to get ahead. All that matters to Zeke is getting what he wants."

"There was a time someone might have said the very same thing about me."

Her voice was quiet, but the words hung heavy in the air. Megan felt Jax stiffen, saw the way his jaw tightened as if he were bracing himself for what she might say next. She didn't want to ruin the fragile understanding they'd been building, but if Jax was going to attend the NA meeting tonight, he needed to leave his cynicism at the door.

"When I was on drugs," she continued, "I did horrible things. Shameful things. Things I knew were wrong, but I didn't care. All that mattered was my next fix."

"Are you comparing yourself to Zeke?" Jax's voice sharpened as his gaze snapped to hers. He jabbed a finger at the arrest record in her hand. "He's a bully, accused of domestic violence—against his own mother, no less—along with a litany of drug charges. According to you, he hit Oliver and used intimidation to get whatever he wanted. People like that don't change, Megan. If anything, they get worse."

"We're all sinners, Jax." Megan's voice was calm, but her words carried the weight of conviction. "We hurt people. Make bad choices. But we're also all children of God. He never stops reaching out to us, no matter how far into the darkness we go. With His guidance, we're capable of change. You've seen the worst in people, but I've seen what happens when they let God into their lives. It's not easy. It's messy and painful, but it's possible."

He was quiet for a long moment. "If Zeke is behind these attacks on you, if he murdered Oliver, then he should be held accountable."

"I don't disagree, but right now, we don't know that he is responsible. And even if he is, that doesn't make him beyond redemption." Megan gently placed a hand on Jax's knee. "If you discover Wesley is behind these attacks on me, would you believe he was beyond forgiveness? Or would you recognize that he's in pain, lost and separated from God?"

He didn't respond. Megan started to pull her hand back, but to her surprise, Jax took it in his. His skin was shockingly warm, his touch gentle as his thumb caressed the edge of her forefinger. Butterflies took flight in her belly. She did her best to quell them down, but it was impossible. The man had an effect on her that couldn't be ignored, no matter how illogical or reckless it was.

"People rarely surprise me." Jax lifted his attention from their hands to meet Megan's gaze. "My dad taught us to be discerning and withhold trust, two things that I carried with me into law enforcement. Working undercover meant making quick judgments. My survival required it. But investigating this case... being around you... I didn't realize how jaded I've become."

Heaven help her, the look in his eyes... her heart skipped several beats. Desperate to hide her true feelings, she lightly pushed his shoulder with her own as her mouth quirked up. "Careful, Detective. It almost sounds like you like me."

He laughed, a low rumble that shifted his features from striking into downright breathtaking. "You know what, Megan?" Admiration sparkled in his eyes when he looked at her. "I think I might, but let's keep that between us for now." Jax winked. "I don't want to ruin my tough-as-nails reputation."

This time, it was Megan's turn to laugh. "Don't worry. I think we're a long way from that." She glanced down at Zeke's criminal record again and the laughter died on her lips. No matter how much she wanted to avoid the truth, someone was hunting her. Either Zeke. Or Wesley. Or a complete stranger. It was terrifying.

How far would the person go to kill her? And why? Megan still didn't even know the real reason she was being attacked.

As if he sensed the train of her thoughts, Jax released

her hand and slung an arm over her shoulder, pulling her against him on the couch. His chest was hard and the strong beat of his heart soothed her. One of his hands still held hers, while the other gently ran up and down the length of her spine.

"It's going to be okay," he murmured, his voice a low rumble that resonated through her.

Megan inhaled deeply, catching the faint scent of Jax's cologne. It wrapped around her like a comforting blanket, slowing her racing pulse. With him, she felt safe. But it couldn't last. The budding friendship they'd formed would melt away as soon as this case was over. There was too much history between them, too much pain, to let it become permanent.

One way or another, this would all end. The only real question was: how?

FIFTEEN

Prince of Peace Church stood in the heart of Knoxville, across from the main square and just down the road from the police department. The building, painted a pristine white, glowed warmly under spotlights that illuminated its steeple, crowned by a simple cross. Behind the church, a smaller building, connected by a covered walkway, housed the conference rooms and pastoral offices. Jax's family attended the Catholic church on the west end of town, but he'd been to a few events here. The pastor, Simon Graham, was Dawson's father.

Jax parked at the curb in the fire lane, positioning his vehicle to face the exit. He'd purposely arrived ten minutes late, hoping to keep a low profile. Judging by the number of cars crammed into the parking lot, there was a decent crowd attending tonight's NA meeting. The thought sent a pang of sadness through him. Addiction touched so many lives. "I didn't realize NA was so popular."

Megan undid her seat belt. "It's the only open meeting for fifty miles, so we get people from out of town too. There are online meetings, but they're not the same. Being here, with other people, makes a difference." She brushed a strand of hair off her forehead, glancing at him with curiosity. "I take it you've never been to a meeting?"

"No." Jax shifted in his seat, his hands tightening on the steering wheel. "Someone suggested Al-Anon when Oliver started using, but..." He let the words trail off, his jaw tightening as shame prickled at the back of his neck. The admission was harder than he'd expected. "I didn't go. Foolishly, I thought Oliver was the one in crisis, so why should I attend meetings to understand addiction? He was the one who needed to fix things. Then..."

Oliver died. And Jax was left wondering if his stubbornness, his pride, and his anger had gotten in the way of helping his brother. The thought gnawed at him, an ache he rarely let surface.

Jax exhaled sharply and stepped out of the vehicle, circling around to the passenger side. Instincts on high alert, his gaze swept over the parking lot before he opened Megan's door. She slid from the seat, hooking her purse over her shoulder. Her bright red coat highlighted the natural flush in her cheeks and complemented her warm brown eyes, but it also stood out like a beacon against the dark night. He placed a protective hand on the small of her back, steering her toward the main doors of the annex.

The sensation of being watched tickled the space between his shoulder blades. Jax stopped and glanced over his shoulder, his hand instinctively brushing the holster at his hip.

No one was there. At least, no one he could see.

Jax breathed a small sigh of relief once they were inside. The warmth of the building hit him first, along with the indistinct murmur of voices from the conference room down the hall. He followed Megan through the entrance, her red coat swaying with each step. They slipped into the room, claiming chairs near the back. As expected, the meeting was already in progress.

The space smelled of coffee. Plastic chairs were arranged in rows with more lining the back wall. A middle-aged woman stood at the front, holding a cup of coffee as she shared her story. Her voice was steady but carried the weight of someone who'd fought hard for every step of her sobriety.

"I lost my family to my addiction," the woman said, her gaze sweeping the room. "My daughter hasn't spoken to me in five years. But staying sober, working the steps, has brought me closer to God and to myself. One day, I hope she'll see that I've changed. I hope she'll give me a chance." She offered a wobbly smile. "But whether she does or not, I'll keep doing the work. Because I deserve to be healthy. I deserve to live a good life."

Applause filled the room as the woman took her seat, and another person stood to speak. It went like that for a while. Each story punctured a hole in Jax's heart until his chest ached, and for the hundredth time that day, he replayed the earlier conversation with Megan. His gaze flickered to the gorgeous woman sitting at his side. She was focused on the speaker, completely unaware that she'd shaken his entire worldview in one conversation.

If you discover Wesley is behind these attacks on me, would you believe he was beyond forgiveness? Or would you recognize that he's in pain, lost and separated from God?

That question had sucker-punched him. Jax had always considered himself a realist. He saw the ugliness in the world and expected it. Megan, however, saw the world through a lens of kindness and hope, always looking for the best in people even when they'd given her every reason not to. Sitting here, listening to the stories being shared, Jax could see why. These people had done terrible things, hurt the people they loved, and yet they were working hard to rebuild their lives. Struggling, failing, picking themselves back up and trying again.

Each of them was worthy of redemption and grace.

It made him think of Oliver.

Jax swallowed hard, his throat tightening. His brother had been in pain. Instead of turning toward God and his family, Oliver had used drugs to numb his pain. Addiction had been his coping mechanism. Would things have been different if Jax had been less angry and more open? If he'd tried to understand instead of judge?

He'd never know. And it haunted him.

When the last person finished speaking, Douglas O'Neal rose from his chair in the front row. The man adjusted his thick-framed glasses before scanning the room and nodding in Jax's direction. They didn't know each other well, but Douglas had been one of Oliver's closest friends in high school—before the drugs drove a wedge between them.

Jax straightened in his seat. He'd never thought to question Douglas about Oliver's accident, since the two of them hadn't been speaking at the time. But maybe Douglas had information about Zeke. Or whether Zeke and Wesley had known each other.

Douglas smiled warmly. "A special thank-you to everyone who shared their story tonight. We have coffee and donuts in the back of the room, so please stay and visit for a while after the meeting is over. To close out, I'd like to invite us all to stand and join hands for the Serenity Prayer."

Jax stood and accepted Megan's offered hand. Warmth spread through him at the simple touch. He tried his best to ignore it, but this persistent connection between them was growing stronger.

Bowing his head, he joined in as Douglas led the group in prayer.

"God, grant me the serenity to accept the things I cannot change, the courage to change the things I can, and the wisdom to know the difference."

A collective "Amen" followed. Applause rippled through the room before people broke off into smaller groups, chatting and laughing as the tension lifted. Across the way, Megan waved at a group of women, and one of them gestured for her to come over. She glanced at Jax.

"Do you mind? I won't be long."

"Go ahead. I wanted to speak to Douglas anyway."

With a killer hunting Megan's every move, time was

of the essence. Jax crossed the room in long strides, catching up with Douglas at the refreshment table. His brother's old friend greeted him with a warm handshake. "Hey, Jax. Nice to see you. It's been a while."

"It has. How have you been?"

"Can't complain." Douglas poured himself some coffee from a thermos, juggling a donut in the other hand.

"Mind if I pick your brain for a moment?"

"Not at all."

Jax led Douglas away from the crowded refreshment table to a quieter corner of the room. From here, he could talk without interruption while still monitoring Megan. Douglas followed his gaze.

"This stuff with Megan... it's crazy," he said, shaking his head. "I'm glad she has someone like you watching her back, but I was surprised to hear you volunteered for the job, considering the history."

Jax tucked his thumbs into his pockets. "It's a long story." He studied Douglas. "How much do you know about the night Oliver died?"

"Only what Megan's told me. I've heard the rumors around town and I know what your family thinks, but there was never any proof she was high that night. People in recovery relapse sometimes, but I don't like assuming the worst. I believed what she told me." His expression darkened, distant. "Still hard though. Megan was driving that night..."

Douglas shook his head, as if pulling himself from a train of thought. "Sorry. I got off on a tangent. What did you want to discuss?"

"I was hoping you could tell me about Oliver's relationship with Zeke Russell."

Douglas's eyes widened behind his thick frames. "Zeke? Now that's a name I haven't heard in a long time. Why are you asking about him?"

Jax hesitated. "He may be connected to the attacks on Megan."

"Well, that wouldn't surprise me. Zeke was violent, and a bit unhinged. I only met him once, but that was enough."

"When did you meet him?"

Douglas took a sip of coffee and grimaced. "You're not gonna like this story. Zeke threw a chair at Oliver once, left a nasty mark on his back. When Wesley found out, he was furious. We drove to Zeke's gym to confront him, and let's just say it got ugly."

Jax's pulse kicked up. He'd suspected Wesley had confronted Zeke about hurting Oliver, but this confirmed it.

"Wesley won the fight," Douglas continued, "but as we were leaving, Zeke swore he'd get even. I was worried, but I should've realized a guy like that was more bark than bite. He was a coward and let others—like Oliver—fight his battles for him." He exhaled, a flicker of regret crossing his face. "After that, I begged Oliver to stop hanging around him. Wesley did too. I wish Oliver had taken our advice. He saved me from bullies when we were kids, and all I ever wanted was to help him."

Douglas's gaze grew distant. "I wish he'd listened to us about a lot of things. Going to rehab. Coming back to church. All of it. But you can't force someone to accept help. They have to want it."

Jax's mind whirled as he processed Douglas's words. Before he could ask another question, Douglas's phone buzzed with an incoming message—just as Megan separated from her group and walked toward them.

"Shoot." Douglas's complexion paled as he read the text. "My mom's been sick all week, and now she says she's having trouble breathing. She thinks she needs to go to the hospital. I have to get over there, but I still need to lock up—"

"We'll do it." Megan gestured for the keys clipped to Douglas's belt loop. "Go take care of your mom."

Jax wanted to argue. Staying behind to lock up after everyone left would leave them vulnerable, but what other choice did they have? He pulled out his phone to message Tucker, who was on patrol. If he could swing by as they were leaving, it'd give them an added layer of security.

"Megan's right, Douglas. We'll handle it."

Douglas shot them a grateful smile as he passed over the keys. "Thanks." Then he hurried toward the exit, tossing his coffee and half-donut in the trash on the way.

"I hope his mom's okay," Megan said, watching him go, concern tightening her features. "She had pneumonia two months ago and was in the hospital for over a week. She hasn't fully recovered."

"Let's say a prayer for her."

Megan's expression softened. "Yes, let's." She took Jax's hand, and together they bowed their heads. "Lord, we ask You to watch over Douglas's mom. Give her the strength to fight off this illness. May she feel the loving touch of Your healing hands. Amen."

Jax lifted his head but didn't let go of Megan's hand. He wasn't ready to lose the connection just yet. The conference room had nearly emptied, only a few stragglers lingering near the exit. He glanced at Megan. "Is there anything special we need to do?"

"We need to pack up the pamphlets next to the door." She gave his hand a small squeeze. "Before we do that, can you tell me what you and Douglas were talking about? It looked serious."

Jax filled her in on their conversation. By the time he was done, the room was empty. Megan absently pulled out a box from underneath the table for the pamphlets. "I didn't know Wesley and Zeke had gotten into a fight. That could explain the photograph left at the crime scene."

Her brow furrowed. "Let's lay it out. Zeke and Oliver get into an argument. Maybe it turns violent. Oliver calls me to pick him up, and when I do, Zeke runs us off the road in a fit of rage. But later, when he realizes he could be implicated, he goes into hiding. Then his gym gets raided because the police were already investigating him and his brother, Cody, for drug trafficking and the illegal fights."

Jax picked up a stack of flyers about the 12-step program and placed them in the box. "Zeke lays low, starts over somewhere else. When the investigation stalls, he figures he's in the clear—until you move back to

Knoxville and I reopen Oliver's case. Now he's scared the truth will come out. So he targets you."

"But he also needs a scapegoat," Megan added. "Wesley is the perfect choice. So Zeke sends me threatening emails before the first attack, setting the stage to point the blame elsewhere. It didn't go as planned, but he still drops the photograph of Oliver, Wesley, and you, trying to muddy the waters. He knows he's going to make another attempt, and he needs the police looking in the wrong direction."

Jax nodded. It fit. Too well.

Megan placed the last of the pamphlets in the box and secured the lid. "But there's still something that doesn't add up."

"What's that?" Jax took the box from her.

"What were Zeke and Oliver doing together in the woods?" Megan flipped off the lights in the conference room and locked the door. The keys jingled in her hands as they made their way down the hall toward the exit. "Why not meet at the gym?"

No one had ever explained why Oliver had been in the woods that night. His car was found abandoned on the side of the road with a flat tire half a mile from the accident.

"Zeke could have lured him out there intending to kill him," Jax suggested, his voice low.

Megan's expression tightened. "That makes sense. Oliver did say someone was trying to kill him when I picked him up. And Zeke is smart enough not to do it at his own gym."

Cold air whipped across Jax's face as he stepped out of the annex and into the night. His truck was the only one in the lot. He'd messaged Tucker, and the officer had promised to be there when they left, but maybe he'd been delayed by an emergency.

"Why kill Oliver though?" Megan twisted the lock on the exit door and then removed the key. "Zeke had a temper, sure, but he wasn't stupid. Oliver was a star fighter. He drew crowds. Zeke was making a fortune off him."

"There are a lot of unanswered questions—"

The scrape of a boot against concrete was the only warning Jax had of another person's presence. He dropped the box. It hit the ground and tipped over, flyers scattering across the walkway. Adrenaline surged. Jax whirled, placing himself in front of Megan even as he reached for his holstered weapon. His gaze scanned the parking lot, searching for danger.

There. A dark shape lurked at the edge of the building.

Someone was out there. Watching.

And Jax knew whoever it was had evil intentions.

SIXTEEN

Fear shot through Megan. Her hand trembled around the keys to the annex as the dark shadow in the parking lot edged closer. Jax pulled his weapon from its holster, stepping back and forcing her closer to the building. An icy wind gusted through the lot, scattering flyers across the pavement. One smacked against her calf, and she nearly yelped before catching herself.

"Open the door," Jax whispered, his eyes locked on the approaching figure.

Megan fumbled with the keys. Her fingers shook so badly she struggled to fit the right one into the lock. Helplessness clawed at her, ramping up her fear. What if the man had a gun? What if he shot Jax? Coming to the NA meeting had been a terrible mistake. And now, they might pay the price.

Finally—praise be to the Lord—the key slid home. Megan turned it with a flick of her wrist just as a voice called out from the shadows.

"Don't shoot." The figure stepped into the floodlight's glow. "I just want to talk."

Megan inhaled. "Cody?"

It had been years since she'd last seen Zeke's older brother, and time had not been kind. Deep pockmarks crisscrossed his cheeks, etched with lines that cut deep into his sallow skin. His thick coat, once sturdy, now sagged on his frame, three sizes too big. A frayed ball cap covered his graying hair, and his left boot had a rip near the toe. He was only forty-five, but he looked closer to sixty.

Drugs? Alcohol? Or something else? Megan couldn't tell, but whatever it was, it had hollowed him out. Once built like a bull, Cody now looked as if a stiff wind could knock him over.

The fear coursing through her dimmed, but she wasn't foolish. Cody lurking in a dark parking lot wasn't reassuring, even if his hands were raised in surrender. His gaze flicked from her to Jax. "Don't shoot me. I only want to talk to Megan."

Jax lowered his weapon slightly but didn't holster it. "Maybe you should try calling first."

"I don't have her number." A violent coughing fit overtook him, rattling his whole frame. He hacked into the grass before drawing a shaky breath. His bloodshot eyes cut to Megan. "Why'd you send the cops to my mother's house looking for Zeke? My brother didn't do anything to you. How could you accuse him without proof?"

The bitter accusation made Megan's stomach twist.

She'd never liked Cody any more than she had Zeke, but it was clear life had beaten him down. She edged out from behind Jax but stayed close to his side. "I didn't accuse Zeke of anything. The police want to ask him about Oliver."

Cody grunted, his attention shifting back to Jax. "I heard the investigation was reopened. Zeke had nothing to do with Oliver's death." His glare swung to Megan. "Everyone knows you killed Oliver. Zeke wasn't even there. Why are you dragging his name into this?"

"If Zeke is innocent, as you say, then he can come forward and tell the police himself." Jax's voice was like steel. "Sneaking up on us in a dark parking lot isn't the best way to defend his honor. How did you even know Megan was here?"

"She runs the NA meetings. Everyone in town knows it."

"How do we get in contact with your brother?"

Cody let out another hacking cough. When he caught his breath, he pressed a hand to his chest. "He moves around a lot. My mom already gave you his number."

"He's not answering."

"Zeke ain't fond of the police."

Jax's gaze sharpened. "Is that because he was selling drugs and operating an illegal fighting ring?"

"Lies!" Cody's pale face flushed with anger. Spittle flew from his lips as he jabbed a finger at Jax. "My brother and I ran an honest business. We worked hard for what we had. But the cops wouldn't leave us alone. They believed rumors from some stupid informant, even after we proved it was all lies."

Megan's posture stiffened. She knew Cody wasn't being honest—she'd seen Zeke selling drugs with her own eyes—but arguing wouldn't get them anywhere. He'd only dig in his heels or lash out. Instead, she focused on something else. "The sheriff's department had an informant? Who?"

Cody's eyes widened, a flicker of panic breaking through his rage. "Doesn't matter. Just leave my brother out of it."

He took a step forward, and Jax immediately shifted in front of Megan, blocking her from view. His grip on his weapon remained firm. "You said what you needed to. Now go."

Cody glared at him. "You think you're better than me, but you ain't. People like you and Megan always get what's coming to you."

Jax's expression darkened. "That sounds like a threat."

Cody didn't reply. His hand drifted toward his coat pocket.

Jax stiffened, raising his weapon. His voice dropped to a dangerous edge. "Keep your hands where I can see them."

Cody froze. Tension crackled in the cold night air as he and Jax held their silent standoff. Megan's breath shallowed, her pulse hammering against her ribs. Then a patrol car turned into the lot, tires crunching over loose gravel as it rolled up to the curb.

Tucker stepped out, his expression sharp with concern. He circled the vehicle, his hand resting on his holster. "What's going on here?"

"Nothing." Cody lifted his hands again for everyone to see. "I was just leaving."

He ambled across the parking lot, humming a tune as he turned down the street toward the north end of town. Megan watched his shadow stretch and shrink under the streetlights until he rounded a corner and disappeared from view.

No one moved until he was gone.

Tucker turned back to them. "Y'all okay? Sorry I was late. Someone reported a prowler in their yard. I had to respond."

"We're fine," Jax said, holstering his weapon. He filled Tucker in on their conversation.

The officer's expression darkened. "I'll follow y'all home. Make sure you get there okay."

They gathered the scattered flyers. Megan's heart was still racing from the encounter with Cody, even after they were on the road toward home. The truck's heater blasted warmth, but it didn't remove the icy block lodged in her chest. She replayed their conversation over in her mind.

"Cody's hiding something." She turned toward Jax. "Noah and Dawson said the sheriff's department raided Bodybuilders because they believed Zeke and Cody were running drugs and an illegal fighting ring. Which they were. But no one mentioned an informant."

"Noah and Dawson might not have known. The

investigation into Bodybuilders was run by the sheriff's department, not ours, so we wouldn't have all the details. The investigators might not have even sent over the files yet. We're not the only department suffering from a personnel shortage."

Megan leaned against her seat. "What if... what if Oliver was the informant? That could explain why Zeke wanted him dead."

Jax nodded. "Same thought crossed my mind. We need those files. I'll text Noah and Dawson when we get home."

The more they uncovered, the more questions surfaced. How did all the pieces fit together? Had Zeke killed Oliver and was now after Megan to ensure her silence? If so, why keep coming after her? The police were already looking for him. Could there be something more to it? Some piece of the puzzle they were missing? Cody's impromptu confrontation suggested there was.

Then again, maybe the two cases weren't connected at all. Zeke may have killed Oliver. And Wesley, believing Megan was guilty, could be seeking vengeance for his brother's death. She prayed that wasn't the case— for Jax's sake—but with Wesley still missing, it was foolish to ignore the possibility that he was involved.

Megan realized she was still clutching the keys to the church annex in her hand. The unyielding metal had pressed deep indentions into her skin. She tucked the keys in her pocket and rubbed her palm. A tremor rippled through her.

Jax reached out, his fingers wrapping gently around her wrist. "You okay?"

His touch was comforting and grounding. Megan drew in a deep breath and grabbed hold of her runaway emotions. "I'm scared. But I'm also tired of feeling weak and helpless." It was time to take charge of her life again, just as she had when she went into recovery. "I don't want to be defenseless anymore. Can you train me? Teach me how to shoot, how to fight back if I have to? If the worst happens—"

"It won't."

He spoke with such confidence. Jax was still holding on to her wrist, and she slid her arm up until their palms touched. The warmth of his skin seeped into hers. Megan interlaced their fingers. This man would take a bullet for her without hesitation, but this wasn't about that. She needed to feel capable and strong. "I still want to learn. Will you teach me?"

He gently squeezed her hand and nodded. "We'll start tomorrow."

"Thank you." Relief unknotted some of the tension in her muscles. Tonight's confrontation with Cody confirmed this was far from over. Megan didn't know what was coming next, but she hoped and prayed whatever it was, she'd be ready for it.

God, give me strength.

SEVENTEEN

Jax studied the target on their makeshift shooting range at the edge of Megan's property. The wind stirred the trees above him, rustling through the dense copse that served as a natural barrier in case any bullets pushed past the stacked hay bales. A few pine needles drifted through the crisp air. Overhead, a squirrel scurried across a low-hanging branch before leaping to another.

"What do you think?" Megan asked, tucking her hands into the pockets of her jacket. Her breath created a fog that vanished into the overcast morning. The deepening shadows in the woods made the lake behind her look moody and dark. "I'm getting better, right?"

Jagged holes punctured the black silhouette on the target. A few shots had strayed from center mass, but most were accurate. A curl of pride stirred in Jax as he shot her a smile. "You're a natural. Most people can't hit a target that precisely after only two days of practice. I'm impressed."

Her face lit up at his praise. "It's because I have such a good teacher."

The compliment twisted something deep in his chest. Spending time with Megan pushed him dangerously close to forgetting why they'd been brought together in the first place. Oliver's death had always been a barrier between them. But now, when he looked at her, the past wasn't the first thing he saw anymore.

He saw a woman who was brave and smart. One with a kind heart and unwavering strength.

A breeze caught a loose strand of her golden hair, sending it fluttering across her forehead. Jax's fingers itched to brush it back, but he resisted. Giving in to this attraction would only lead to heartache for them both. Instead, he focused on replacing the target. "Want to practice some more?"

She adjusted the zipper on her coat and nodded. "Then I'd like to go over the moves you showed me yesterday." Turning, she strolled toward the front of the shooting range.

Without warning, Jax grabbed her from behind, locking one arm around her neck and securing it with his other hand. Megan gasped as he lifted her off her feet. She scrambled to put her legs underneath her, and the moment they touched the ground, she tilted her body weight toward his elbow. Her shoulder shoved against his chest as she wrenched herself free and bolted.

"Nice job!" Jax called out as he caught up with her. She was breathless, her cheeks flushed, a smudge darkening her chin. Guilt punched him hard. He brushed her hair aside to get a better look at her neck. The strands were silky against his fingertips, but all he could focus on was the redness of her skin. "I'm sorry, Megan. That was too rough."

"No." She placed a reassuring hand on his chest. "If someone tries to hurt me, they'll be a lot rougher. You just caught me off guard, that's all." A grin broke across her face, her brown eyes sparking with accomplishment. "I got away, though."

"You did."

Their gazes caught. Held. Jax suddenly noticed just how close they were to each other. One more step and Megan would be in his arms. The cold had put a pretty flush in her cheeks and her lips were coated with a shimmery gloss that drew his attention to her mouth. His pulse hammered against his ribs. His breath stalled. Unconsciously, his thumb brushed against the curve of her jaw.

She inhaled. Beneath his fingertips, which lingered along the delicate column of her throat, Megan's heartbeat jumped. Jax knew he should back away, but couldn't bring himself to do it. He was frozen—unable to move forward, unable to give in to the insane desire to kiss her.

A crow cawed overhead, its sharp cry slicing through the moment.

Megan blinked. She took a step back, dropping her hand from his chest. "I should..." She trailed off, glancing at the shooting range. "Practice. I should practice shooting."

"Right." Jax struggled to regain his equilibrium. He

handed her a set of headphones and put on his own. For the next few minutes, he watched as Megan repeatedly fired the handgun at the target. Her grip was firm, her stance steady. When she was done, more of the bullets had landed dead center.

Jax removed the target from the hay bale. "That's enough for today. Let's grab something to eat. I'm starving."

She chuckled. "You're just looking forward to Pops's brisket."

"You got that right." Jax's mouth watered at the thought. Clay's slow cooker had been working all morning, the scent of hickory and mesquite hanging in the late afternoon air.

They gathered their things, including Jax's personal handgun that Megan had been practicing with, and headed toward the house. Grass crunched under their boots. Jax's gaze swept over their surroundings. It had been two days since the confrontation with Cody, and Megan's attacker hadn't struck again. But Jax wasn't taking any chances. Not even with Special Forces still guarding the property. He knew this wasn't over. The killer was planning his next move, and it was only a matter of time before he struck again.

"I've been thinking a lot about the night Oliver died." Megan pushed aside a branch on a small sapling. "Trying to remember any detail that might help figure out what happened."

Jax glanced at her, surprised by the sudden shift in conversation. "And?"

"Nothing. There are holes in my memory. That's not uncommon when something traumatic happens, but I can't shake the feeling that I'm missing something important—some key piece of the puzzle." She exhaled in frustration. "I can't live like this forever, Jax. My boss, Tess, called me this morning. Douglas's mom is in the hospital, so they're down another counselor. Tess has canceled as many appointments as she can, but I'll need to go back to work soon. My clients need me."

Jax wasn't thrilled with the idea of Megan going back to work before her attacker was caught. "Let's give Noah and Dawson a little more time. They're still working on tracking down the list of Zeke's friends you gave them. The divers recovered the drone from the lake, so tracing the purchase might lead them to whoever's behind this. I know it's frustrating, but police work is slow and tedious."

Wesley was also still missing. Jax had convinced his parents to file a missing person's report, and now every law enforcement officer in the country was on the lookout for his brother. That Wesley still hadn't been found bolstered Jax's theory that he was in the wilderness somewhere, trying to work through his PTSD or memories of being a prisoner of war.

At the start of all of this, he'd been angry with Wesley for taking off and leaving them in this position. Now, all he felt was sadness. His brother was hurting and trying his best to handle that pain. The coping mechanism might not be the healthiest, but what Wesley needed was grace and understanding. Something Jax had learned from attending the NA meeting with Megan.

He glanced at the gorgeous woman at his side. "I've been meaning to ask you. The NA meetings... are they always open?"

"On Tuesday nights, yes." She pushed another branch aside. "Thinking of going again?"

"Maybe. Hearing those stories... it was eye-opening. And I've been thinking a lot about how I've been processing Oliver's death." The words felt heavy, but keeping them bottled up wasn't working. If anyone would understand, it was Megan. "I've been blaming myself. I helped raise Oliver and Wesley. My dad worked oil rigs, my mom pulled double shifts at the factory. I was the one who made sure they got to school, did their homework, ate dinner. When I left for college... it was a relief. For the first time, I could focus on myself."

Megan slipped her hand into his, a simple, steadying gesture that encouraged him to keep going.

"When Oliver's friend died, he started spiraling. I came home and tried to talk to him, but he wouldn't listen. He rebelled against every piece of advice I gave him. It made me mad." Shame pressed against his rib cage. "I didn't want to deal with it. Selfishly, I wanted to keep living my life."

She squeezed his hand. "That's not selfish."

"It feels that way."

"Because our minds play tricks on us. They convince us we're responsible for things that were never ours to carry." She slowed, then stopped completely, forcing Jax to do the same. Turning to face him, her gaze searched his. "You need someone to say this out loud to you: What happened to Oliver wasn't your fault. You couldn't have stopped him from making bad choices. I know it's easier to blame yourself than to blame Oliver because he's gone, but that doesn't make it right."

Her words hit like a sledgehammer to his chest, knocking the breath from his lungs. The weight of them pressed down, so heavy it felt like his heart was bleeding. He clenched his jaw. "But what if..."

"You could have saved him?" She shook her head, her voice gentle but firm. "No, Jax. You can't solve every problem or take the blame for every wrong. Oliver was eighteen. Old enough to make his own choices. He knew drugs were a mistake. Yes, he was hurting, and he deserved grace, but that doesn't change the fact that he rejected help over and over again. That's not your fault. Nothing you could have said or done would've changed that. Addicts only get help when *they're* ready. Not a minute before."

Jax swallowed hard, emotions clawing at his throat. "He died before he could."

"Yes, he did. And that hurts. I know." She stepped closer, wrapping her arms around his waist and pulling him into a hug. Her head rested against his chest. "I'm so sorry, Jax. I know you loved him. And I know you miss him."

He shattered. Right there, in the woods on her property, under the shelter of a large oak tree. Jax's heart broke into a thousand sharp pieces that ripped through the angry scar tissue he'd built over his grief. Tears flowed down his cheeks. There was nothing he could do to stop them. Instead, he wrapped his arms around Megan. She held him up, weathering the storm of his sorrow until the worst had passed.

When it was over, she released him and reached into the pocket of her coat, unearthing a package of tissues. She handed him several. Heat crawled up his neck as he swiped at the tracks on his cheeks. Jax wasn't emotionally barren, but he couldn't remember the last time he'd cried. Maybe when he was six.

"Sorry. I don't know what just happened." He cleared his throat, grasping for his dignity. "I didn't even cry at Oliver's funeral."

"Then that was long overdue, I'd say." Megan wiped a tear from her own cheek. Then she shoved his shoulder. "Don't worry, you can still keep your man card."

He huffed out a laugh. "I'm not sure you get to decide that, being female and all."

"Probably right." She looped her arm through his, leading them back toward the house. "Come on. We've got brisket to eat."

His stomach rumbled in agreement, drawing another laugh from her. But just as they stepped out of the trees, a whirring noise sent Jax's heart rate into overdrive. His gaze shot skyward.

A drone was approaching.

EIGHTEEN

Megan's body ran cold with fear when she spotted the flying bug-like object heading straight for them. It was still too far away to see if a weapon was strapped to the bottom, but she didn't need a closer look—she already knew the answer. And in that moment, a terrifying realization hit her. All her target practice had been in vain. Had she truly believed she could shoot a drone out of the sky? Or, worse, take down an actual person if it came to that?

Jax grabbed her hand, pulling her back under the cover of the trees. His gun was already in his grip. "Get low."

She dropped to the dirt, pressing herself beneath a thick bush. Through the gaps in the leaves, she could just make out her house in the distance. Her heart pounded with fresh panic and the roar of her pulse filled her ears. "My grandparents?"

"Kyle's got them covered."

Even as Jax spoke, Megan spotted the former Army security specialist sprinting across the yard. He ducked inside the house, securing Nana and Pops. A second later, Jason and his German shepherd, Connor, approached their location. With a sharp command, Jason ordered Connor to take cover. If the drone opened fire, the dog would be defenseless.

Connor weaved his way through the trees, heading straight for Megan. He plopped down beside her in the dirt, pressing close. She buried her fingers in his thick coat. The German shepherd seemed to sense her fear, nudging her hand as if to reassure her.

The drone's buzz grew louder. Jax crouched beside her, gun raised, his hand firm on her back. Fear gripped her, thick and suffocating.

She didn't want anyone to get hurt.

Especially not Jax.

The handgun case rested next to her other hand, where Jax had dropped it. Megan grabbed it but didn't bother opening it. Paper targets were a lot bigger than a flying drone, and the last thing she wanted was to create a distraction. Jax and Jason had training. They knew what they were doing. She had to trust them—and follow orders—even if it left her feeling helpless.

The advice Sandy, her sponsor, had given a few days before rolled through Megan's mind. *When life feels overwhelming, take it moment by moment. Breathe. Pray. Remember—you're not fighting this battle alone.*

A strange stillness washed over her, pushing back the panic threatening to take hold. Megan inhaled deeply, grounding herself in the moment. The feel of the cold earth beneath her, Connor's warm body beside her, the steady weight of Jax's hand on her back. The crisp scent of pine filled her lungs. She wasn't alone. She wasn't powerless.

God, I put my trust in You. Protect Jax and Jason, my grandparents, Kyle. Give us the wisdom and strength to do what's right—no matter what comes next.

The prayer steadied her. Unlike before, fear didn't paralyze her—it sharpened her focus. The drone buzzed overhead. Through the thick foliage, she caught only glimpses of its dark frame, but then the wind shifted, revealing a clear view of the weapon strapped to its underside.

Not a flamethrower this time.

An assault rifle.

"He can't see us," Jax murmured.

The drone hovered, its camera swiveling, searching. The seconds stretched, unbearably long, until—finally—it veered away, speeding toward the lake.

Relief crashed over Megan.

"Let's go." Jax tugged her to her feet. Then he turned to Jason. "I'll get Megan to the house. See if you can find the pilot."

"On it." Jason's face hardened, all sharp angles and battle-honed focus. Sunlight caught the scar on his left cheek. He gave a quick command to Connor, and the German shepherd leapt to his side. In a blink, they vanished into the trees.

"We have to run, Megan. The house provides more

safety, but we have to get across the yard before the drone comes back." Jax's words were clipped and hurried. "I need you to focus on getting to the house. Don't worry about anything else. Got it?"

Her gaze swept over the long expanse of the yard, separating their hiding spot from the house. Fear clawed at her chest, threatening to take hold, but she forced it back. She could do this. She *would* do this. Their lives depended on it. Jax would never leave her, and the longer they stayed out in the open, the greater the risk that someone would be hurt.

She met Jax's gaze. His expression was calm and controlled, but in the depths of his dark blue eyes, she recognized the fear. Not for himself. For her. Without thinking, Megan rose onto her tiptoes and brushed her lips across his. The kiss was featherlight, but it sent a shockwave through her system.

Then she turned on her heel and did as Jax instructed.

She ran for the house.

NINETEEN

The next morning, Jax sat on the Ingles's front porch, bundled against the icy cold as he watched the sky lighten with the rising sun. Sleep had been elusive. He wasn't sure if it was the case or the memory of Megan's kiss that had kept him up all night. Either way, he was bone-tired, on edge, and utterly confused. Not even a long run on the property had cleared his head.

Tires crunched over the driveway as a Knoxville Police Department vehicle arrived. Dawson climbed out, carrying two takeaway cups of coffee. His boots thumped against the porch steps. "Morning." He handed over one of the coffees. "Triple expresso. Figured you'd need all the caffeine you could get, considering you texted me at three in the morning."

Jax grunted and took a sip of the dark brew, but not even that could cut through the fog in his brain. "Megan survived yesterday's drone attack by the grace of God, but the killer isn't letting up. We still don't know who is behind this or even why she's being targeted."

Jason and Connor had attempted to apprehend the drone pilot, but he'd escaped before they could. A neighbor reported seeing a dark blue or black Explorer parked on a dirt road around the time of the attack, but he had thought little of it—people often used that path for fishing.

No description of the driver. No license plate numbers.

They had nothing. More than a week into the investigation, and they were still no closer to uncovering the truth. It was demoralizing. Frustrating. Terrifying. Jax had designed layers upon layers of protection for Megan, and still, it almost hadn't been enough. If the drone had flown lower... if the shooter had fired indiscriminately... things could have gone very differently.

Dawson tossed his cowboy hat onto the small table before settling into a rocking chair, stretching his long legs in front of him. The stillness of the morning settled around them, broken only by the chirping of birds waking from slumber. It should have been soothing. Instead, it only heightened Jax's anxiety.

He slanted a glance at his old friend. "What aren't you telling me?"

Dawson twisted the coffee cup in his massive hands. He was dressed for work in BDU-style pants and a thick jacket. A crisp wind swept across the porch, ruffling his light brown hair, and a muscle in his jaw twitched. "We located the purchase order for the drone you shot down.

The one that was pulled from the lake. Wesley bought it six months ago, shortly after moving back to Knoxville."

The news hit Jax like a punch to the chest. His grip tightened around the coffee cup. "That's impossible."

"Is it?" Dawson sighed. "I know you don't want to hear this—I don't want to be saying it—but Wesley has always been the primary suspect in this case. He has the means, the motive, and the capabilities of pulling something like this off. Zeke's involvement never made much sense."

"What are you talking about? The man has practically disappeared off the face of the planet."

"True. We tracked down all the friends Megan told us about. No one has heard or seen from Zeke in ten years, except for his family. That's strange, I grant you, but Zeke has no real reason to come after Megan now. Especially if he's living somewhere else under a new name. Attacking her would only draw more attention to him, not less." Dawson leaned forward, resting his elbows on his knees. "We're pursuing two cases at once. Oliver's accident and these attacks against Megan. There's never been proof that the same person is responsible for both."

"So what? You think Zeke ran Oliver and Megan off the road and then just disappeared?"

"I think it's likely." Dawson grimaced. "We finally got the files from the sheriff's department. Oliver was an informant for them, just as you suspected. I think Zeke found out somehow and attacked Oliver."

Jax's chest clenched. It should have made him feel better to learn his brother had turned Zeke into the police, but with Wesley as the prime suspect in these attacks against Megan, that news barely registered.

"Oliver got away," Dawson continued. "He called Megan and asked her to pick him up. When she did, Zeke ran them off the road. He knew the sheriff's department would suspect him, so Zeke fled town. Cody was questioned. Nothing came of it. I'm not sure he knew what Zeke had done."

"He does now."

"Yes." Dawson's mouth flattened into a thin line. "That's why he's worried about us searching for his brother. He doesn't want Zeke arrested for murdering Oliver."

Jax exhaled sharply. "So how do we know for sure Cody isn't the one coming after Megan?"

Dawson shook his head. "The man has lung cancer. He's far too weak to have pulled off the first attack on Megan." He shot Jax a knowing look. "Cody's guilty of protecting his brother, but that's not a crime."

Jax rose and crossed the wide expanse of the front porch. Trees lined the horizon, leading down to the road that stretched toward town. Dawn had fully come, painting the earth with a warm glow that made a dent in the frosty temperatures. He still felt as cold as ice crystals clustered on the grass though.

"Two cases, Jax. Two different perpetrators. Zeke is likely involved in Oliver's death, and we're pursuing that lead. As for the attacks on Megan are concerned..."

"You think Wesley is behind them."

Dawson sighed. "We have to follow the evidence.

First, there was the photograph dropped at the first attack —it indicates a family connection. Now we have proof that at least one of the drones was purchased by Wesley. It's no secret your family blames Megan for Oliver's death, and your brother hasn't been himself since returning home."

Jax's hand slipped into the pocket of his jacket. The original photograph was in evidence, but he'd made a copy. Oliver's face smiled brightly from the center of the picture, and every day since the first attack, Jax had stared at the brother he'd lost. Today, his attention was drawn to Wesley's image. So young... so trusting. He fingered the edge of the picture where it had been ripped, right through his own younger face.

His brother had bought the drone. The revelation was both shocking and horrifying. Coupled with the photograph, it was clear why his colleagues suspected Wesley. Still, Jax couldn't accept it. "Wesley wouldn't do this. I know how it looks, but..."

He couldn't find the words to defend it. A knot of stress twisted his insides, sending a sharp ache through his stomach. Megan's neighbor spotted a dark-colored Explorer on a dirt road near the time of the drone attack. "Zeke has a black Explorer registered in his name. Wesley doesn't. He has a truck."

It was weak logic. Explorers were a popular SUV, and they were common in Texas.

"Wesley could have rented it. We're looking into that." The rocking chair creaked as Dawson rose. "I pray I'm wrong about this, Jax. I really do."

The words were sincere. If anyone could understand his inner turmoil, it was Dawson. They'd spent most of their twenties and early thirties in separate cities on different career paths, but it hadn't diminished the deep friendship forged during childhood. Dawson knew how much Jax loved his family.

He glanced down at the picture again. "Will Wesley be arrested?"

"He's still only a person of interest at the moment. Chief Garcia wants to question him first before we move forward."

Jax exhaled. Chief Garcia, Dawson, Noah—the entire force was composed of the best cops Jax had ever worked with. He needed to trust them to do their job.

After Dawson left, Jax lingered on the porch, staring at the photograph of his brothers. It didn't offer any answers. His coffee cold and his fingers frozen, he turned with a sigh and went back inside the warm house. Music drifted from the kitchen. A piano piece, soulful and somehow uplifting. Jax followed the sound, unsurprised to find Megan sitting alone at the kitchen table.

She didn't notice him at first. Morning light streamed in the window, caressing the delicate lines of her face. She was so beautiful... like a painting. The memory of their kiss yesterday flashed like a lightning bolt in his mind. It was followed by a storm of conflicting feelings. They hadn't discussed the kiss yesterday, both of them pretending as though it hadn't happened.

But it had. And Jax didn't know what to do about it.

Megan must have sensed him watching, because she

turned. "Good morning." She averted her gaze, a wrinkle of concern crossing her forehead. "I saw you with Dawson on the porch, but didn't want to interrupt. It looked like a serious conversation."

"It was."

His words hollow, Jax filled her in on their discussion. The music changed from a haunting piano piece to something more upbeat. He reached over and flipped off the radio, letting silence settle over the kitchen. The pipes in the old house groaned— Clay and Rose were awake, starting their day. Jax busied himself by making a fresh pot of coffee for them.

He sensed rather than saw Megan rise and move closer. Before she could touch him, he shook his head. He didn't want comfort. Not now. Not when he was barely holding it together. "I'm okay. Noah and Dawson will do their job."

Megan was quiet for a long moment. Then, softly, she said, "You're allowed to believe your brother is innocent."

"I know that." Jax snapped the lid onto the coffee canister and braced his hands on the counter. "But what if I'm wrong? I've been mistaken before. I was about you."

"Then you cross that bridge when you get there. Until then..." Megan wrapped an arm around his waist, leaning her head on his arm. "Hold on to hope." She tilted her face to smile up at him. "And eat chocolate. Lots and lots of chocolate."

He chuckled, tempted to plant a kiss on her adorable nose. "For breakfast?"

"Yep. We can make chocolate chip pancakes." She grabbed a mixing bowl from the drying rack next to the sink. "Nothing soothes the soul like carbs and chocolate, coated in maple syrup. I'm convinced calories don't count when you're running for your life from a deranged killer. Or, in our case, a weapon-enhanced drone."

"Fair enough."

Jax opened the fridge, pulling out ingredients as Megan listed them off. Despite everything pressing down on him—the case, the danger, the uncertainty—he relaxed as they argued over which recipe to use and fished out egg shells from the batter.

"You definitely didn't inherit your grandmother's cooking abilities," he teased.

Megan tried to scowl but dissolved into laughter. "I know. I'm hopeless. Once, I tried to make brownies and ended up burning them. Nana has practically forbidden me from cooking alone."

Jax took the whisk from her and nudged her aside with his hip. "Allow me." He mixed the batter, adjusting the consistency with a splash of buttermilk. Pancakes had been a weekend staple growing up, something he'd made for his brothers when their mom worked double shifts.

Megan watched with admiration. "You're a pro."

"I don't know about that, but at least we won't end up with burned pancakes."

She flicked a bit of flour onto his shirt before dancing away, laughing when he reached to retaliate.

A few minutes later, Clay and Rose entered the kitchen, and the space filled with warm chatter and the rich scent of fresh coffee. The easy rhythm of cooking, the jokes, the laughter—it all helped chase away the lingering worries.

For a little while, he let himself enjoy the moment.

Then, just as they sat down to eat, Megan's phone beeped with an incoming message. She scanned the screen, her smile fading.

She glanced up at Jax, worry tightening her features. "We have a problem."

TWENTY

Megan's fingers flew over the keyboard as she transcribed notes from her last client session. The door to her office was open, allowing the background hum of support staff to filter in from the hallway. A quick glance at her watch confirmed it was almost four. The day had flown by.

"I'm almost done," she murmured, glancing at the loveseat tucked in the corner of her office. Jax sprawled across it, his long legs hanging off one end, his broad frame making the small furniture piece look even more diminutive. A cowboy hat covered his face, shielding his eyes from the overhead lighting. His breathing was deep and steady.

Poor guy had passed out. She couldn't blame him. Spending hours at Clearview Counseling, shuffling in and out of her office between client sessions, had to be mind-numbing. But Jax had insisted on staying. For her protection. His steady presence had allowed her to focus on clients instead of worrying whether her attacker might strike again, and for that, Megan was grateful.

It'd been a hectic day.

Tess, Megan's boss, had come down with the flu. Douglas's mom was still in the ICU. That left the counseling center short-staffed, and although the office manager had rescheduled as many patients as possible, there were still a few appointments that couldn't be postponed. Megan had fretted about leaving the safety of her property, especially after yesterday's drone attack, but so far, the day had passed without incident. She prayed it would stay that way.

A knock on the doorframe pulled Megan from her thoughts. She glanced up to find Stacey, the receptionist, wringing her hands. Her gray-streaked hair was pulled back from her narrow face, and a pair of reading glasses hung from a chain around her neck.

"I'm sorry, Megan, but we just had a client walk in. Quinton Jones. I told him Douglas isn't here today, but he's insisting on speaking to someone." Stacey bit her lip. "I can tell him to come back if you need to leave, but... he seems distraught."

Quinton. Megan mentally grimaced, remembering their last interaction at the coffee shop, where he had asked her—point-blank—if she had killed Oliver. Quinton normally saw Douglas. She could insist he wait until her colleague returned, but if Stacey thought he was upset, could she send him away just because she was uncomfortable?

She accessed his records on the computer, scanning

through the notes. "Douglas hasn't updated anything in Quinton's file for months." Megan glanced at Stacey. "Any idea what the issue is?"

"He wouldn't say, but it looks like he's been crying."

That was all Megan needed to hear. "Send him back, Stacey."

Stacey nodded and disappeared down the hall.

Their conversation had interrupted Jax's nap. He sat up, rubbing his face, and Megan shot him an apologetic look. "Looks like I'll be a bit longer."

"It's okay." He stretched as he stood. To preserve their privacy, Jax couldn't stay in the office while she spoke with her clients. "I'll be in the hall if you need me."

Megan grinned, gesturing toward his chin. "You've got a little drool there, Detective."

A faint blush crept across his cheeks as Jax wiped at his face, only to realize a second too late that she was messing with him. He shot her a playful glare.

Megan chuckled, setting her legal pad and pen on the small table in the seating area. "You know, in action movies, the hero never sleeps. What if something happened while you were napping? *I* would've had to save *you*."

"Trust me, sweetheart, my eyes were closed, but no one would get past me to you."

Megan's breath hitched. *Sweetheart?* She turned, but Jax had already disappeared into the hall.

They'd both been dodging the elephant in the room since she'd recklessly kissed him yesterday, but obviously, he was thinking about it too. That knowledge both exhilarated and terrified her. She didn't want to survive these near-death incidents, only to have her heart broken by Jax.

And broken is what it would be.

There was no future for them. Megan was a part of the worst day of his life. That fact couldn't be erased, no matter how much she might wish otherwise.

A shadow filled her doorway. Quinton. His long-sleeved shirt strained against his broad chest and muscular arms. Mud peppered the bottom of his jeans, and his scuffed boots suggested he'd paid little attention to where he'd been walking. His ball cap was turned backward, dark hair curling at the edges. And, just as Stacey had said, his complexion looked rough—eyes red, jaw tight.

Despite his imposing size, Quinton reminded her of a broken little boy.

Megan waved him toward the couch and shut the office door. "What's going on, Quinton?" She sat down across from him. "You seem upset."

He wouldn't meet her gaze.

Megan let the silence stretch, giving him time to gather his thoughts. Finally, he swallowed hard. "If someone asks you to do something... something wrong... but also right... what should you do?"

Megan settled back in her chair. "That sounds complicated. Can you tell me more?"

He licked his lips, nervous. "I..." His eyes flicked up to hers, then away again. "Maybe this isn't right. I was hoping to talk to Tess."

"Tess is out sick with the flu." Megan offered him a reassuring look. "I know you were expecting her, and I'm sorry she's not here to help. But I am. It's clear something is weighing on you. Let's talk about it. Maybe we can figure this out together."

He trailed a finger across the stitching of her couch. "That guy out there... he's a cop, isn't he? He's protecting you. I heard about the attacks. Everyone in town is discussing it."

I'm sure they are. Megan hadn't been out and about town since the first drone attack, but her imagination filled in the blanks. Gossip about her had run rampant before all of this. It would take months to die down, but eventually it would. Right now, the rumor mill was the last of her concerns.

No, her primary aim at the moment was Quinton. Clients sometimes latched onto irrelevant topics to avoid discussing what was troubling them. "We aren't here to talk about me, Quinton." She kept her voice calm but firm, setting a boundary. "I want to understand what's bothering you, but you have to tell me what's going on. If you don't want to talk, we can end the session now."

His gaze snapped to hers. "That's rude."

Anger colored his words. Goosebumps prickled across Megan's skin, and her gaze shot to the closed door. Jax was right outside.

Calm down. There was no reason to be afraid of Quinton. He was struggling with whatever he needed to say, and she was just on edge from the recent attacks.

"It's not my intention to be rude," she said evenly, her

patience thinning. Maybe he needed to ease into the conversation. "Why don't we start with what you did today?"

Quinton's leg jittered. "I bought a gun," he blurted.

She stilled. "What kind of gun?"

"Does it matter?"

"I suppose not." Megan once again glanced at the door. She resisted the urge to get up and open it. "Why did you buy a gun?"

He swallowed hard, his leg bouncing even more. "I've been asked to do something, and I don't know if it's right." His breath hitched. "I..." Quinton shook his head and abruptly pushed to his feet. "This was a mistake."

"Wait." Megan replayed their conversation in her head—his tears, his hesitation, his anxiety. Dread churned her stomach. "Quinton, has someone asked you to do something illegal?"

He shook his head quickly, but the gesture wasn't convincing. "I shouldn't be talking to you—"

"Why not?"

He didn't answer. Before she could utter another word, Quinton bolted for the door.

Megan sprang from her chair and chased after him. "Quinton!" She heard Jax's footsteps behind her, his voice cutting in with a sharp, "What's going on?"

There wasn't time to explain.

An internal whisper told Megan she had to stop Quinton before he made a terrible mistake. Desperation quickened her steps. "Quinton, wait! Please!"

He didn't slow. Quinton raced past Stacey's desk,

ignoring the receptionist's startled question, and shoved open the main door. Cold air hit Megan's face as she followed him outside. A black Explorer revved its engine, tires screeching as it tore out of a nearby parking space. Quinton was behind the wheel.

She waved frantically, trying to get him to stop.

He didn't.

"Megan!"

Jax's strong arm wrapped around her waist, yanking her back just as the Explorer whipped past, narrowly missing them. The vehicle peeled out of the lot and disappeared onto Main Street.

Megan stood frozen in Jax's grip, her breath coming in short, uneven gasps.

"What just happened?" Jax demanded.

"He..." Megan nearly blurted out the whole incident before catching herself. She couldn't confide in Jax. Patient-client confidentiality applied. She replayed the conversation in her head. Quinton's behavior had been erratic, and Megan suspected someone had asked him to do something illegal, but she didn't have confirmation. Her legal and moral obligation was with her client. "I can't tell you what Quinton said. It's covered by confidentiality."

Jax's brow furrowed as he stared down the road. "He was driving a black Explorer."

"Is that important?"

"I don't know." Jax's gaze settled on hers. "A neighbor spotted a dark-colored Explorer on a dirt road near your house around the time of the drone attack yesterday."

His words sent a chill down her spine. "Lots of people have black Explorers." She struggled to keep the worry at bay. Could Quinton be responsible for the attacks on her? Or was she seeing danger where there wasn't any? None of this made sense. "I need to speak to Douglas."

Megan hated to bother him with his mother in the hospital, but she needed to understand the gravity of the situation. Since Quinton was normally his client, Douglas should have a better handle on whether there was reason to be concerned.

She hurried back into her office and scooped up her cell phone. Scrolling through her contacts, she found Douglas's number and clicked her screen to dial it. He didn't answer. Frustrated, Megan left him a message explaining it was an urgent client matter and asking him to call her as soon as possible. She tossed the phone on her desk. A headache was brewing behind her eyes.

"Can you tell me anything?" Jax circled the desk and sat on the corner.

She shook her head, collapsing into her leather chair and leaning against the headrest. "No. I'm probably over-reacting."

There was nothing in Quinton's file to indicate he was violent. He'd been a drug user, but had been clean for nearly a year. At least, according to the records she'd read. Douglas hadn't updated them in a while. That bothered her, but it wasn't uncommon. He'd never been very good at keeping up with his paperwork.

Megan sighed. "Hopefully, Douglas will call soon.

He's at the hospital. Some ICUs don't allow cell phones, depending on their rules."

Jax opened his mouth, about to ask something else, but his phone buzzed. He pulled it from his pocket, glanced at the screen. Then he shot to his feet.

Megan went back on high alert. "What is it?"

He blinked as if he couldn't quite believe what he was reading. "They found my brother. Wesley is at the police station."

TWENTY-ONE

The Knoxville Police Department buzzed with activity. Uniformed officers hunched over cubicles, hammering out reports, while a steady hum of voices mixed with the occasional ringing phone. The air carried the faint scent of sweat and stale pizza, though the place itself was remarkably clean—except for the bearded man slumped on a bench in county-issued jail clothes. His wrists were cuffed in front of him, and from the look of his greasy hair and dirt-streaked face, he hadn't showered in days.

Jax barely noticed any of it. His gaze was locked on Chief Garcia's office door, his pulse thudding like a war drum. Inside, his boss and Noah were questioning Wesley. The blinds were drawn, blocking his view.

Was his brother about to be arrested for attempting to kill Megan?

"Dude, chill," Dawson muttered. "If you keep pacing in that same spot, you're gonna wear a hole in the floor next to my desk."

Jax stopped mid-step and shot him a glare. "You really want to start on me right now?"

"No. I'm just saying, if you need to pace, maybe take a lap around the building instead of breathing down my neck." Dawson scowled. "I can't focus."

Instead of taking his colleague's advice, Jax leaned over the cubicle wall. He needed a distraction. "Did you find something on Quinton Jones?"

"Nothing that would indicate he's responsible for the threats against Megan. He's from Dallas, but has been living in Knoxville for the last several years. Works as a welder for a local construction company. He's been arrested in the past for drug possession, but they were minor charges. Nothing in the last year. Quinton rents an apartment on the north side of town. Owns a 2006 Ford Explorer." Dawson leaned back in his chair. "He's too young to have known Oliver."

"I wouldn't assume Megan's attacker knew Oliver." Jax planted his hands on his hips. "Oliver's death and the reopened investigation have been in the local news for weeks. Quinton could have decided to take matters into his own hands."

Dawson arched a brow. "And he just happened to be carrying around a decades-old photograph of you and your brothers?"

Jax clenched his jaw. Good point. It didn't add up. His gaze flicked back to Garcia's office door. His muscles remained tense and his insides were knotted. What was taking so long?

Megan emerged from the break room carrying two

bottles of water. Her dark-purple dress was cinched at the waist with a simple belt, accenting her natural curves. Knee-high black boots and a blazer kept the look professional, but that didn't stop the jolt of awareness from hitting him square in the chest. His world was in chaos, but the minute Megan came into view, something shifted. He felt grounded. It was unlike anything he'd ever experienced before.

Dawson hummed low in his throat. "Man... you got it bad."

Jax was going to kill his friend. Murder him right there in the center of the police station. "Shut. Up." He couldn't even wrap his head around these developing feelings for Megan. The last thing he needed was commentary about the complicated mess he found himself in.

Megan joined them. Her dark brown eyes held a mix of warmth and worry as she offered Jax one of the water bottles. "Here. I thought you might like something to drink." Her gaze flickered to the chief's closed office door. "Nothing yet?"

"No." Jax's heart pinched tight as he took the water. Megan's life had been threatened repeatedly over the last week, maybe at the hands of his brother, yet here she was checking in on him. It wasn't right. He placed a hand on the small of her back and escorted her a few steps away from Dawson's desk so they could speak privately. "I'm sorry. I haven't even asked if you're okay. This is hard on you too."

"I'm fine. Just worried about you." She placed a hand

on his chest, right over his heart. "I've been saying a lot of prayers, asking for God's guidance. Maybe I'm not the right person to offer comfort in this moment, but..." Her gaze lifted to his. "I care, Jax. And I hope and pray that everything works out. For you. For Wesley. For all of us."

Her compassion undid him. Jax knew it wasn't wise to nurture these feelings for Megan, but he didn't have the strength to harden himself against them. He covered her hand with his. Megan's skin was soft against his fingertips and he lost himself in her gaze. She gave him hope. Without realizing it, she reminded him to lean on his faith, that goodness still existed, and that he shouldn't let jadedness take over his thinking.

He drew in a breath, lightly scented with Megan's perfume, and felt the tension ease from his body. His thumb rubbed across the backs of her fingers as his gaze dropped to her lips. She leaned in, just enough to make his heart slam against his ribs. A magnetic pull drew him closer...

Dawson appeared at his side. "Jax, your parents are here."

His words hit like a bucket of ice water.

Jax tore his attention away from Megan, the noise of the police station yanking him straight back into reality. He dropped her hand and stepped away, aware that his closeness to her would spark a firestorm. Dawson grimaced in silent apology before stepping aside to reveal Greg and Valentina Holt. And in an instant, Jax knew it was too late.

His parents had seen him. With Megan.

Valentina appeared shell-shocked, her eyes wide and confused. His dad, on the other hand, was stone-faced. His glare could've melted the skin off Jax's face. The fact that they were in a police station was likely the only reason Greg contained his temper.

Guilt swallowed Jax whole, thick and suffocating like quicksand. He took a cautious step forward. "Mom, Dad—"

"Not a word," Greg growled. His voice was low, tight with contained rage. The tips of his ears burned red, his posture stiff as iron. "Not. One."

The sharp rebuke drew Jax up short. He wasn't a little kid any longer, but somehow, his dad still had the power to make him feel three feet tall.

Before he could find his footing, the door to Chief Garcia's office swung open. Noah stepped out, his gaze landing on Jax. The detective's expression gave nothing away, but he nodded in reassurance and then said, "We're done. Jax, the chief would like a word with you and your family."

Greg didn't say anything—just turned on his heel and stalked into the office, Valentina trailing behind. Jax followed at a slower pace, pulling in a deep breath before shutting the door behind him.

His gaze locked on Wesley.

His brother looked—and smelled—like a man who'd spent more than a week in the woods. An unruly beard covered the lower half of his face while premature gray peppered his hair at the temples. His military-style boots were coated in mud. Fishing lures hung from a pocket of his cargo pants. Wesley stood, arms crossed over his broad chest, feet planted in a wide stance. He looked every bit the soldier, ready for battle.

Chief Garcia rose from the chair behind his desk. "Please everyone, take a seat. I'm sorry for making you wait, but we had some issues to discuss."

"I imagine so." Greg's tone was harsh, and while Valentina took the offered chair, his father remained standing. "My son hasn't done anything wrong, and I'd like to know why he was hauled in here like a criminal."

"No one dragged me in like a criminal, Dad." Wesley's tone was even and respectful. "I was stopped by police at the state line and informed that Chief Garcia needed to speak with me, so I drove straight here. Long story short, I've been camping at the Ozark National Forest. I've provided receipts from gas stations and supply stores, along with my recently acquired Arkansas fishing license."

He lifted his chin. "The drone that was purchased in my name isn't mine. My identity was stolen about six months ago. I don't know by whom, but they opened a couple of credit cards in my name. I filed a police report with the sheriff's office and have given a copy of that to Chief Garcia."

The chief nodded. "Everything checks out. At this time, we don't have any reason to believe Wesley is involved in the attacks against Megan Ingles."

Jax exhaled, his knees going weak with relief.

Wesley's expression tightened as his attention zeroed in on Jax. Hurt flashed in his eyes before it was masked behind a shield of armor. "You actually believed I had something to do with it."

He shook his head. "Wes—"

"Don't." Wesley's jaw flexed, his voice tight with restraint. "I spent the last ten days in the middle of nowhere, fishing, hiking, minding my own business. I come back to town and discover my own brother—someone who should know me better than anyone—thought I was capable of attempted murder."

Valentina sat silently in the chair, her fingers twisted in her lap, her eyes darting between her sons. Jax opened his mouth, but Greg didn't give him a chance to answer.

"You put that woman above your own family." His father's voice was low, vibrating with contained fury. "We lost Oliver, and instead of standing with us, you're off defending the very person responsible for his death."

Jax felt his own anger ignite. His father's grief was like a raw wound, but that didn't make his accusations true. He met Greg's heated glare head-on. "She didn't kill Oliver. They were run off the road. If you let the investigation finish, then I'm sure it'll prove—"

"Do you hear yourself?" Greg's hands curled into fists. "You don't know what it's like to bury a child, Jax. You don't know what it's like to live with the kind of grief that makes you want to scream every single day." His voice wavered, just slightly, before he pulled himself together again. "All I know is that Oliver was fine until she came into his life. And now he's gone."

Jax's chest ached. He understood his father's pain. He did. But it didn't change the truth.

"I miss him too, Dad," Jax said, his voice thick with emotion. "But blaming Megan won't bring him back. Catching the person who ran them off the road won't fix our pain either. Nothing we do will bring Oliver back. He's gone."

A broken sob escaped Valentina as she buried her face in her hands. Greg's anger didn't waver, but his touch was gentle as he placed a comforting hand on his wife's shoulder. Then, pinning Jax with a hard stare, he said, "You've developed feelings for that woman, and it's blinding you to the truth."

"No, Dad. We've let out grief turn into anger, and it's eating us alive. Do you think this is what Oliver would have wanted for us? Do you think this is what God wants for us? This isn't who we are."

They were making the same mistake Oliver had—drowning in their pain. Instead of seeking support from each other and grieving together, they were channeling their heartache into a wall of hatred. A different coping mechanism, but just as destructive.

Jax turned to his brother. It was time for some hard, honest truths. "I'm sorry. I never thought you were guilty, but I won't lie and say there were moments of doubt. You've locked me out. You've locked all of us out, hiding away in your cabin and leaving town for days on end without any way to contact you. I don't know what you've been through. I won't pretend to understand. But I also won't apologize for being scared about your well-being."

Wesley exhaled slowly, his expression unreadable,

but Jax could see the war happening behind his brother's eyes. For a moment, it seemed like he might say something—might let his guard down—but then his jaw tightened. He turned to Chief Garcia, his voice flat. "Are we done here?"

The chief nodded. "For now."

Wesley didn't say another word as he walked out of the office. Greg hesitated for only a second before helping Valentina—still shaking with quiet sobs—out of her chair. Without another glance in Jax's direction, he followed their youngest son out the door. The sound of his mother's quiet weeping lingered in the room.

Jax felt like he'd just been ripped in half.

And somehow, he had a sinking feeling that the worst wasn't over yet.

TWENTY-TWO

Firelight flickered across the living room, casting warm shadows along the floor. Megan curled her legs beneath her on the couch, her untouched tea cooling at her elbow. Instead of drinking it, she ran her fingers over the scrawled letters in the margins of her father's Bible.

You are never alone. God is always with you.

Her gaze drifted to the window. Jax was out there, walking the perimeter. They hadn't spoken much since returning from the police station. Noah had told her Wesley was cleared of all suspicion, so she'd expected Jax to be relieved. Instead, he'd been distant. Whatever had been said in the chief's office had hurt him deeply, and she didn't know how to help. So she prayed.

"Megan."

She looked up to see Nana standing in the arched entryway, her hair in curlers, her nightdress and robe swallowing her petite frame. In her hands, she held a cup of tea. "I'm going to bed, sweetheart. There's fresh coffee on the stove and a plate of sandwiches in the fridge for the Special Forces boys on duty tonight."

Megan nodded. Her grandmother shuffled across the room on slippered feet and brushed a kiss against Megan's head. The move made her feel small. Tears she hadn't known were banked rose to the surface. If Rose was startled by them, it didn't show. Instead, she set her tea down and gathered Megan in her arms. "Oh, sweetie."

"I don't know why I'm crying." The tears fell fast and hot.

"Well, you've been through the wringer these last few days." Nana pulled some tissues out of a box on the side table before handing them to Megan. "But if I had to guess, I'd say these tears might have something to do with a certain tall, handsome detective."

She blotted her face, a flush rising in her cheeks. "Is it that obvious?"

"Sweetie, a blind, deaf mule would realize the two of you have feelings for each other."

Megan let out a watery laugh, but the weight pressing on her chest remained. "I kissed him. We haven't talked about it, and things have been weird ever since. Then today, his family saw us together at the police station and..." She bit her lip. "I'm not responsible for Oliver's death, but I was there when it happened. That's a history you don't just move past."

Nana sat beside her, taking her hands in her own. "No, you don't move past it, honey. But you can move through it." She gave Megan's fingers a gentle squeeze.

"You don't have to pretend those memories don't exist, and neither does Jax. The past is part of who we are, but it doesn't have to define where we're going. You know that better than anyone."

Megan nodded. She was a firm believer that your past didn't determine your future. People could make different choices. Better ones. "So, you think I should be honest with him?"

"Yes. Love, even when it's complicated, even when it's messy, is still a gift. If Jax is meant to be in your life, you'll find a way. And if he's not..." She tucked a loose strand of hair behind Megan's ear. "Then you'll still be okay."

Megan swallowed past the lump in her throat and hugged her grandmother. "How do you always know the right thing to say?"

Nana chuckled. "It comes with age, along with the creaky joints and the gray hair." She rose and collected her tea, kissing Megan one more time. "Goodnight, sweetie."

"Night."

Nana shuffled out of the living room, leaving Megan alone with her thoughts. The fire crackled in the hearth, the flames licking at the logs, twisting and flickering in an almost hypnotic rhythm. She stared into them and her mind drifted, as it often had this week, to the night Oliver was killed. A rush of fear came instinctively, but this time, she didn't fight against it. She let it wash over her. Let herself become immersed in the memories.

The dark country road. The blur of the forest flying past.

Oliver, jumping out from behind a tree, wild-eyed and frantic.

The slam of her brakes.

When he'd climbed into the car, he'd smelled of hay and sweat, his hands trembling as he gripped the dashboard.

Drive. He's going to kill me. Drive!

His panic had been overwhelming. Megan tried to remember everything he'd said, but it was a jumble. Still, there was something—something buried deep in her memory. A crucial detail just out of reach. She could feel it, hovering on the edges of her consciousness, but no matter how hard she tried, couldn't pull it free.

A hand landed on her shoulder.

Megan screamed, springing from the couch like a startled cat. She whirled to face her attacker with fists raised.

Jax stepped back, his palms facing outward in a paci-fying gesture. The firelight flickered along the hard planes of his face. "It's just me."

She pressed a hand to her chest, her heart hammering against her ribs. "Good grief, Jax. You scared the daylights out of me." She forced her other hand to relax. "I almost punched you."

His lips twitched. "I noticed. All those self-defense lessons have paid off." He tilted his head. "I called your name three times. What were you thinking about?"

Her shoulders slumped. "The accident. There's

something about it I can't remember, and it's bugging me." Megan bent to retrieve the Bible that had fallen to the floor, along with the blanket, when she'd launched off the couch. "I was watching the fire and didn't hear you come in at all. Sometimes flames can have a hypnotic effect."

Jax took the Bible from her, smoothing out a creased page. He smelled of the cold outdoors and something distinctly him. Water droplets peppered his hair, darkening the strands.

Belatedly, Megan heard the rain hitting against the window panes. She shivered, thinking of the men guarding her property. "Walker and Logan are on duty tonight. They don't need to stay out in the rain. I'll tell them to come into the kitchen."

She moved to go around Jax, but he caught her hand.

"Don't. They're okay. They brought clothes for the weather."

His touch sent a shock wave of heat through her system. When he didn't let go, Megan stepped closer, tilting her head up to look at his face. He was breathtakingly handsome. She studied each strong line, from the masculine curve of his upper lip to the sweep of his cheekbones. And then his gaze clashed with hers. The stormy blue held a mix of emotions she couldn't decipher.

Without a word, he cupped her face. His thumb traced her cheek and then his fingers slid into her hair. He tilted his head until their foreheads touched. "Megan..."

"Shush. I know." She stepped closer into the circle of

his arms. Jax didn't need to explain. She'd already figured out that he cared, but his family hated her. He didn't have any more answers than she did.

And right now, for just this one second, she didn't care.

She wanted to forget about everything. The threats on her life. The accident. The men guarding her property in the rain and her grandparents sleeping in the next room. Instead, she focused on the beat of her heart and the feel of Jax's hand on her waist. His breath whispered against her lips. She tilted her face toward his and, a second later, was lost.

This was not the kiss in the trees, a brief runaway moment of recklessness. This was something else entirely. Jax's mouth claimed hers with a slow, deliberate intensity, like a man who had finally stopped fighting what he wanted. His lips were warm, his touch sending waves of heat through her. There was no hesitation, no second-guessing. Only raw, unfiltered need wrapped in something deeper—something that stole the breath from her lungs.

Megan pressed closer. She felt the rhythm of his heartbeat beneath her fingertips. It pounded in time with hers. Jax kissed her like she was something precious. Something he couldn't bear to lose. And she answered with everything inside her. The longing. The hope. The quiet fear that this moment might be all they ever had.

It shocked her. The depth of their connection. When the kiss ended, Jax looked as stunned as she felt. He swallowed hard, but didn't release her. "That wasn't smart."

"No." Her breath was ragged. "But it was honest."

His lips curled into a shadow of a smile before pressing against hers once more. Then he pulled her into his arms. Megan rested her head against his chest, her eyes closing as she soaked in the warmth of his embrace. His shirt was soft beneath her cheek, and the way he cupped the back of her head—cradling her like she was invaluable—made her heart ache in the best way.

It'd been a long day. A confusing one. But Megan couldn't let it finish without saying what was in her heart. "I care about you, Jax. I might..." She breathed out. "I might be falling in love with you."

His body tensed for the briefest moment before relaxing. He exhaled, then pressed a soft kiss to the top of her head. "I can't go against my family, Megan. Right now—"

"I know. It's okay."

Silence settled over them, broken only by the crackling fire. Megan didn't want the moment to end, but knew it had to. With God all things were possible, but it would take a miracle for her and Jax to find a way forward. She pulled away. "It's late. I should go to bed."

Jax nodded. It looked like he wanted to say something, but then he tucked his hands in his pockets. "Night."

Megan turned and started up the stairs, but an idea struck her mid-step. She paused on the landing. "Jax." Her voice was a whisper, but he still heard her and came around the corner. "The accident. I've been trying to remember everything that happened, but can't. Whatever it is, I know it's important."

The police suspected Zeke was the one who ran them off the road, but Wesley had been responsible for the threats against her. Now that Wesley had been cleared as a suspect, it left them floundering. Who was trying to kill her, and why? Was it Zeke? Or someone else?

Jax had always believed the cases—Oliver's death and these attacks on her—were connected. Megan did too. Figuring out what happened that night would require her to be brave and face one of the worst experiences of her life. But it was the only way to unlock her memories.

Rain beat against the roof. The storm wouldn't last. Megan knew they had a small window to put her plan in motion. "I have an idea."

TWENTY-THREE

Headlights cut through the inky night, illuminating sheets of rain as they pelted the asphalt. Jax tightened his grip on the steering wheel, his gaze flicking to the rearview mirror. The country road stretched behind them, empty. For the hundredth time since Megan had shared her idea, he second-guessed this plan.

"Are you sure about this?" His eyes shifted from the mirror to Megan. She sat tucked into the passenger seat, dressed in a ski cap and dark gray rain jacket.

"Dawson and Noah have tracked down every lead they can, and nothing has helped. We still don't even know if Zeke is the man after me, or if it's someone else. I'm done being afraid. Running from my memories of the accident has only made things worse. I want to do everything I can to figure out what happened that night. Sometimes revisiting the scene of an accident can help with memory retrieval and trauma processing. It allows the brain to reconsolidate the memory in a way that might bring clarity." She turned to face him. "That's why we have to do it now. At night, in the rain. I want the conditions to be as close to the same as possible."

Jax admired her bravery, but this move bordered on recklessness. He hadn't spotted any sign of a tail, but the storm was coming down hard, making it impossible to know for sure. Noah had agreed to meet them at the accident site with the case file, but even that didn't settle Jax's nerves.

He checked the mirror again—still nothing—then tapped the brakes to slow for the turnoff onto the narrow country road. Towering trees flanked either side, their rain-heavy branches sweeping together overhead, forming a dark tunnel.

Beside him, Megan stiffened.

Jax eased the SUV to a stop. He reached for her hand without thinking, his need to protect her outweighing any desire to uncover the truth about Oliver. What he'd said earlier in the chief's office was true—finding out what happened that night wouldn't bring his brother back. Nothing could. But Megan was alive. And vulnerable. She had to come first.

"You don't have to do this, sweetheart." Jax knew the accident site would be difficult for him to revisit, and he hadn't been in the car crash. Megan had been pushed to the emotional brink this week. She was strong, but her grandfather's warning rang in Jax's ears: *everyone has a breaking point.* "Noah and Dawson will figure it out. It may take them time, but they'll get there."

She met his gaze. Half of her face was cast in shadow,

the other side illuminated by the light from the dashboard. Megan smiled and squeezed his fingers. "I know you want to protect me, but I'm strong enough to do this. I wasn't always. But I am now."

His heart tumbled over. Megan was the heady mix of sweetness, brains, and fortitude. Kissing her this evening had unlocked the truth Jax had tried desperately to bury. He was falling for her too. But saying so, admitting the words out loud, would only hurt them both. After everything his parents had been through, Jax refused to pour salt on their wounds.

There was no future for him and Megan. No matter how much Jax wished otherwise.

He leaned over and brushed a kiss on her lips. Soft and tender. Then he squeezed her hand. "Okay. Let's do this."

Megan straightened in her seat. "I'm going to talk through it. Saying things out loud can help...." She stared out the window into the night. The headlights illuminated the wet road and the wild overgrowth on either side. "I was driving slowly, worried that I'd miss Oliver. He didn't give me a specific meeting point. Just told me he'd be waiting somewhere near the fallen tree after the bend."

"That's coming up." Jax slowed. The road curved and an oak tree, toppled in a previous storm, listed precariously close to the road.

"Stop here," Megan ordered. She reached into the pocket of her raincoat and pulled out her cell phone. "I tried calling Oliver, but he didn't answer. His phone went straight to voicemail, like it'd been turned off or he didn't have good signal. I waited here for what seemed like forever, but was probably only five minutes. It was cold. My sedan didn't have good heating, and the storm was gaining intensity. I was worried about hail or tornadoes. At the same time, I didn't want to leave Oliver out here in the woods. He'd sounded so scared on the phone. So desperate."

Her voice caught, barely a hitch, but Jax heard it.

His chest clenched. His instinct was to reach out—to comfort her—but doing so might break her concentration. "Oliver's car was found half a mile away with a flat tire. Did he say anything to you about that?"

"No. I learned that later." She let out a long exhale. "When Oliver didn't show up, I kept driving a little farther down the road."

Jax eased off the brake, letting the SUV roll forward. They passed the fallen tree, the windshield wipers sweeping away the rain as a dirt road turnoff appeared in the headlights.

"Stop!" She pointed to a cluster of trees on the left. "There. That's where he came from. Oliver was soaking wet. No jacket. His hair was plastered to his head, like he'd been out in the storm the whole time. There was a scuff on his chin, like he'd been in a fight. It looked fresh, but I dismissed it at the time."

"Makes sense. He was often involved in fights for Zeke." Jax frowned, thinking back on the official reports. Megan was right. Oliver had been dressed in jeans and a long-sleeved shirt that night. No jacket. It was a small detail, but it mattered. "His jacket wasn't in his car either. Investigators assumed that Oliver's tire went flat, and that's when he called you. But his car was half a mile from here. Assuming he came here to meet someone..." Jax shifted in his seat, looking at the thick forest surrounding them. "It's raining. It's cold. No one would stand around in a storm."

"He smelled like hay when he got in my car." Megan inhaled sharply. "There's a barn at the end of that dirt road. Oliver was the one who showed it to me." She hesitated and then admitted, "We used to get high there. Have parties sometimes."

Jax had forgotten all about the barn. "Oliver used to go there as a kid."

"What if he met Zeke there? Or if not Zeke, the person who attacked him?"

Jax's mind raced as childhood memories surfaced. "There's a trail that cuts through the woods to the barn. Based on where Oliver's car was found, he must have taken that path." Frustration burned through him. "When I surveyed the scene after joining the police department, the path was overgrown. I didn't remember it was there until now."

Megan wasn't the only one with buried memories. Jax's heart pounded against his rib cage. They were on the cusp of figuring out what had happened to Oliver. He could feel it. Tomorrow morning, at first light, they would get a search warrant for the barn. Ten years had passed, but it might still contain clues that would lead them to the killer.

Jax drummed his fingers against the steering wheel. "Whoever Oliver was meeting with, the arrangement was made in person. There was nothing in his cell phone records." He glanced at Megan. "Oliver drives here. Parks his car. Walks the path to the barn to meet someone."

"But something goes wrong." Megan picked up his train of thought. "There's an altercation. Oliver gets a scrape on his chin and loses his jacket. Runs away and calls me, begs me to pick him up."

"Why you?" Jax had asked that question many times during the investigation. "He had other friends. You and Oliver hadn't spoken in months. Why reach out to you?"

"I've been thinking about that. Oliver was an informant for the sheriff's department. He'd turned on Zeke, which meant turning on everyone in that world. Maybe he was worried that no one else could be trusted."

It made sense. "You weren't a part of that circle anymore."

"No. I dropped all of those friends when I got sober." Megan ran her hands over her jeans and breathed out. "Oh Jax, what if he was going to get clean? We talked about it months before. I told him life would get better once he got off drugs, that I'd help him. Oliver didn't accept my offer at the time, but I felt like he heard me. So much so, I thought he'd call in a week or two."

His heart stuttered. Jax didn't know if it made things worse or better to realize that his brother may have finally decided to straighten out his life. He swallowed hard. "It makes sense he was considering it. Especially if he was feeding information to the sheriff's department about Zeke." Jax stared at the empty road and the woods beyond. "But he was high at the time of the accident. So maybe that's just wishful thinking."

"I'm sorry." Megan's hand came to rest on his arm. "Maybe I shouldn't have said anything."

"No. It's better you did. We don't know which details are important and which ones aren't." He tossed her a reassuring look. "This is good. We're making progress. Let's keep going." His gaze flicked back to the cluster of trees where Oliver had hidden that night. "What happened after he got in your car?"

"He was panicked. He yelled at me to drive. Told me someone was trying to kill him." Megan pointed down the road. "I went that way. The rain was beating against the car and Oliver was shouting..." She bit her lip. "I couldn't follow everything he was saying."

Jax eased off the brake again, and the truck rolled forward. A part of him hated bringing Megan back to the crash site, but he recognized it might dredge up a memory that would crack the case wide open. "When did you see the headlights behind you?"

"Not until they were right on top of us." She hugged her arms around herself as the woods along the left side of the road thinned, revealing a steep drop off into a drainage ditch. "The truck rammed us, and I screamed. It was hard to keep my sedan on the road. Oliver..." Her eyes widened as she inhaled sharply. "Oliver said, I never should've trusted him. He's going to kill us."

"He could've been talking about Zeke. You said the vehicle was a truck. Are you sure?"

She frowned. "I remember thinking it was a truck because of its size, but... it could've been an SUV. Maybe even a van."

That fit. Zeke had an Explorer.

"Oliver was yelling at me to drive faster." Megan's voice was hollow, like she was lost in memories. "Then he grabbed the wheel. I fought him for control, and that's when the truck rammed us again." She swallowed hard. "And then... we went off the embankment."

Jax brought his SUV to a stop. Even after ten years, some of the trees still bore the scars from the crash—deep gouges in the bark where Megan's sedan had torn through them before plunging into the ditch. Rainwater rushed through the culvert below, not deep enough to swallow a car, but enough to have half-submerged the front of her Toyota that night.

Megan reached for the door handle. A second later, she was outside, standing on the side of the road, staring down at the ditch. Jax shoved the SUV into park. Rain smacked the top of his cowboy hat and slid down the collar of his jacket. When he reached Megan, his chest clenched at the look on her face.

Pain. Grief. Heartache.

A mirror of his own emotions. He reached for her, raising his voice to be heard over the storm. "Megan..."

"I couldn't save him. I tried, Jax. I tried so hard." She let out a choked sob. "For years, I thought it should've been me who died. Some part of me still does."

"No!" He stepped in front of her, blocking her view of the ditch, and lightly grabbed her forearms. Her raincoat was slick against his bare hands, her slender form curved inward, weighted down with a decade of guilt. Jax shook her slightly, and Megan raised her face to meet his desperate gaze. "I'm grateful you survived. Do you hear me? What happened wasn't your fault. It wasn't my fault. It wasn't even Oliver's fault. The only person responsible for what happened is the man who ran you off the road."

Lightning streaked across the sky, sending a fresh shot of adrenaline through him. Thunder rumbled in the distance. They needed to get out of the storm. Jax guided her back to the truck, securing her inside before making a careful three-point turn. The wind shoved at the vehicle like invisible hands as they headed away from the crash site.

Megan hadn't said a word. Her blonde hair clung to her face in damp tendrils, rain mixing with the tear that tracked down her cheek.

Jax reached across the console and took her hand. "I'm sorry. I shouldn't have brought you here—"

"No." Her chin trembled. "I didn't realize... I didn't know how much I needed to hear that."

"That I'm grateful you survived."

Megan nodded, her lips pressed together as if she was holding back a wave of tears. She shifted closer, as much as her seat belt allowed, and rested her head against his arm. "Thank you, Jax."

He pressed a kiss to the top of her head, then let his cheek linger there for a moment. That centered feeling washed over him again. The push-pull of their relationship, the way each of them bared their soul to the other... there was safety and love and respect.

He didn't feel alone. Not in his grief, not in his anger, not in his heartache. But it was more than that. Megan saw him. He'd had girlfriends in the past that were easy to be around when things were light. But when tough times came, they bailed. Megan was the first person he could laugh with, and the first person he could cry with. He could be himself.

And that realization brought with it another powerful truth.

He was in love with her. Not falling in love. Not possibly in love.

In love.

Headlights flickered on the road ahead. The storm made it difficult to see, but the vehicle was big—an SUV or a truck.

Megan sat up. "There's Noah."

Jax's muscles stiffened. His foot eased off the gas. Noah was supposed to meet them out there, and it was likely his vehicle heading their direction, but logic didn't silence the whispered warning running through Jax.

"Megan, get down in your seat—"

A burst of gunfire shattered the windshield.

TWENTY-FOUR

Pebbles of shattered glass rained down on Megan.

Her heart slammed against her ribs as bullets tore through the SUV's front end. She'd ducked at Jax's command, and the move had saved her life. Frigid air and rain howled through the gaping windshield as she fumbled with her seat belt, her trembling fingers slipping against the latch. Finally, it released. She slid down into the wheel well, pressing herself into the smallest space possible.

The SUV lurched in reverse, tires skidding against the slick road as Jax maneuvered them away from the gunfire.

Her gaze snapped to him. He was shouting into his phone, his voice raw with urgency, while simultaneously steering through the storm. Dash lights illuminated his face. Raindrops clung to his lashes, trailing over the hard edges of his jaw, where dark stubble shadowed his skin. Determination powered every movement. Megan had never been more terrified in her life, but she knew, without a doubt, Jax would do whatever it took to keep her safe.

He tossed the phone in the cup holder. "Megan, are you hit?"

"No." The answer came automatically, but then she did a quick scan of her body. Adrenaline could be masking an injury, but she didn't feel any pain. She was okay. Her gaze traveled the length of Jax's torso, and a fresh jolt of fear shot straight through her.

Blood dripped from his jacket sleeve, trailing over his fingers.

Her stomach bottomed out. "You've been shot!"

"I'm fine." He gritted his teeth. The truck hurtled backward, but another sound cut through the chaos—the sickening thump-thump of rubber slapping against asphalt.

They had a flat. Maybe two.

Jax let out an uncharacteristic curse. Then, without warning, the vehicle jerked sideways. Megan was thrown against the door, her skull knocking against the hard surface. Pain splintered through her head, a brutal reminder of the stitches still holding together the wound from the first attack in the woods.

Shivers wracked her body. From the cold. From the pain. From the fear.

Trees closed in around them as the SUV jolted over rough terrain. Jax had veered onto a dirt road. He yanked the wheel hard, and the vehicle shuddered before finally jerking to a stop.

Jax killed the lights, plunging them into suffocating darkness. Megan heard his door open and felt rather than saw him move. A moment later, the passenger side door flew open. Jax was a dark silhouette against the storm.

"Come on." His voice was urgent. "We have to run."

Run? Where?

Megan scrambled out of the truck, her boots sinking into the mud. The storm made it impossible to see more than a few feet ahead. Wind tore through the trees, rain slashing sideways. Lightning split the sky in a jagged streak, followed by a boom of thunder so powerful it rattled her bones.

Headlights swept across the dirt road.

The shooter was coming for them.

Jax grabbed her hand. His palm was slick with rain and blood. Together, they bolted into the woods. Wet branches slapped Megan's face and roots threatened to trip her as she struggled to keep up with Jax's breakneck pace. Her breath came in ragged gulps. Traversing the woods in the dead of night reminded her of the first attack. Panic threatened to overwhelm her, but Megan battled it back. She wasn't alone. Jax was with her. Falling apart would put his life at risk by slowing them down. She would never do that.

She was strong. And God was always with her.

Help us, Father.

Jax suddenly lurched to the side, his hold on her hand slipping. Megan caught him just as he stumbled.

Lightning blazed across the sky, making the woods as bright as a summer day. Jax's face was ghost pale and twisted with pain. Blood ran like a river down his hand. In the other, he gripped his gun. He raised it and fired into the woods. Then he grabbed her hand again.

Bark exploded beside Megan. She screamed and ducked, barely able to catch her footing as Jax yanked her deeper into the forest. She couldn't hear anything over the pounding of her own heartbeat and the rain, but it was clear the killer was following them. And closing in fast.

Jax veered to the left, and a clearing appeared. An ancient barn loomed. Overgrowth climbed the broken boards, giving the impression that the earth was trying to take back the structure. Rain slicked over the steel roof. Jax pulled her across the clearing. Megan struggled to keep up, her shoes sliding in the thick overgrowth. Snakes and ticks crossed her mind. She tossed the thought away. There were far deadlier things in these woods tonight.

A door swung violently on its hinges, slamming against the side of the building with each gust of wind. Jax released her long enough to grab it, gesturing with his gun-wielding hand for Megan to go inside.

She bolted through the entrance. Birds in the rafters stirred at the unwelcome intrusion. The air was thick with the scent of mold, damp earth, and rotting hay. Water dripped from her soaked raincoat onto the cracked cement floor. Behind her, the door slammed shut. She spun just as Jax wedged a wooden beam through the handle to barricade it. It wouldn't hold the shooter back for long, but it would buy them a few precious minutes.

Jax yanked his phone from his pocket. The screen

glowed, revealing the call from the truck was still connected. "We're in the barn. Noah, can you hear me?" He glanced at the screen and growled. "No signal."

"How far away is he?"

"Five minutes. Dawson is with him, but it'll take them time to reach the barn from the road." Frustration bled into his voice. "The shooter was wearing night vision goggles. Even in this storm, he won't take long to track us. Especially if he's been here before."

"There's a place we can hide." Megan grabbed Jax's arm, forcing his attention to her. Then she spun on her heel, heading deeper into the barn. She flicked on her phone's flashlight to illuminate the way.

The old structure groaned under the storm's assault. Wind howled through the rafters, rattling the tin roof. Rain dripped from holes overhead, pooling around bales of hay stacked haphazardly against the far wall. Something skittered across the floor, and Megan clapped a hand over her mouth to stifle a scream.

A mouse darted into the darkness.

She swallowed her revulsion and pushed forward. The horse stalls ended, revealing a row of doors. One led to an office, another to a tack room. Dust coated every surface.

She yanked open a third door. Rusted hinges groaned in protest.

The stockroom.

A workbench stretched along one wall, nails protruding from the rough-hewn planks above it held rusted tools. Cobwebs hung from the ceiling, swaying in the draft. The air was thick with decay and mildew. Her breath fogged in front of her as she pointed to another door at the back of the room. "That's an exit."

Jax brushed past her to check. He cracked it open, peered into the night, then shut it again before securing the lock. He turned to Megan, exhaustion and pain etched deep in his face. Even so, he managed a reassuring smile. "You did good, sweetheart. A room with an entrance and an exit."

She took no comfort in his compliment. Blood dripped down his hand, staining the dusty concrete floor dark red. Jax was bleeding badly, and judging from the paleness in his complexion, he was running on strength of will and adrenaline.

Her gaze swept the room. She spotted a battered stool and dragged it away from the workbench. "Take off your jacket and sit down."

"I don't—"

"Sit, Jax." Her tone brooked no argument. "You're no good to me if you pass out from blood loss."

To her relief, he didn't argue. He moved sluggishly, struggling to pull his jacket off his injured arm. Megan helped him. Blood had soaked through his shirt, the fabric clinging to his skin. The bullet had torn through his shoulder, likely nicking an artery.

Urgency fueled her. She shed her raincoat, then her sweater, leaving only the cotton button-down underneath. Cold air kissed her skin, raising goosebumps as she fumbled with the buttons. She grabbed a rusted knife from the workbench and sliced through the fabric, tearing it into makeshift bandages.

Bundling one into a ball, she pressed it against the wound.

Jax hissed, his body going rigid.

Megan winced. "Sorry. Hold this here."

He set his gun down on the bench and pressed his uninjured hand against the fabric. She balled up another piece and pushed it against the exit wound on the back of his shoulder. Working swiftly, she wrapped strips of her shirt around his arm, binding the makeshift bandages in place. Jax clenched his jaw as she tightened the last knot. Sweat beaded on his forehead, but he didn't utter a word of complaint.

To her relief, the bleeding slowed. He still needed a hospital—maybe even surgery—but at least he wouldn't keel over right here.

Megan touched his cheek, tenderness washing over her. "I think you'll live."

He rose, capturing her mouth with his. His lips were cool to the touch, and the kiss was brief, but it packed a punch. Megan felt dizzy from the rush of it. Then she shivered as he moved away from her, picked up his gun, and peeked into the barn through a hole in one of the wooden beams.

Birds in the rafters fluttered. Megan's heart rate shot into the stratosphere as a creak followed. Was someone in the barn? She grabbed a crowbar from the workbench. The weight of the cold metal was reassuring. It wouldn't help her in a fight against a bullet, but it was better than nothing. Then she flicked off the flashlight on her phone.

Darkness swallowed them. Fear stole her breath. Gripping the crowbar, she eased back toward the exit door. Her back bumped against a wooden storage ledge. The rotting beams caved under her slight weight, and Megan stifled a gasp as she toppled to the floor. Pain shot through her body as she collided with the hard cement.

Heaven help her, had the killer heard that?

Shock and fear froze her in place. She held her breath, her gaze locked on Jax's back. He stood at the ready, gun pointed at the door. Several long, tense breaths followed. Then Jax eased open the door to the storage room and stepped into the main area of the barn. His boots scraped against the cement as he returned. "No one's there."

Megan breathed out a sigh of relief and scrambled to her feet. She flipped her flashlight back on. The beam flashed across something on the floor. She stifled a scream and stumbled back, straight into Jax's arms. Pieces of rotting wood littered the cement where she'd fallen into the feed ledge. The makeshift box had shattered.

Among the wreckage, lying in the dust and decay, was a human skull.

TWENTY-FIVE

Megan trembled against him. She clutched the crowbar as if it could shield her from the bones scattered on the floor. Jax eased her aside and crouched down to examine the remains. The skull had a giant hole in the back. A bullet wound, if he had to hazard an educated guess.

The body had been here a while. Long enough for bugs and scavenger animals to pick the bones clean, despite the fact that it'd been stuffed in a storage ledge. Tattered clothes clung to the skeleton. A jacket and blue jeans. Among the rotting wood and bones was a wallet. Using the barrel of his gun, Jax flipped it open.

His body went ice cold as he read the name on the driver's license.

Megan crouched beside him. Her light vanilla perfume was a welcome relief from the stench of the decay and mold. She gasped. "It's Zeke." Megan shook her head. "That's impossible. I don't... I don't understand."

Jax's mind raced as he struggled to make sense of everything he knew. Pain from the bullet wound, and the subsequent blood loss, clouded his thinking. "He never answered our calls. No social media. No job history. No one has seen or heard from him in ten years—not his friends, not his neighbors. Only his family."

Cody's warning came rushing back. *Leave Zeke alone.* His threats. His desperation.

Jax exhaled. "Cody's been cashing Zeke's military disability checks. Maybe splitting the money with his mother. That's why they never reported Zeke missing. It's also why they didn't want us looking for him."

Megan blinked. "But... if Zeke has been dead all this time, then who's been trying to kill me?"

Jax's pulse hammered as everything snapped into place. "The cases were always connected—Oliver's death and the threats against you." The puzzle pieces that had refused to fit before were shifting, aligning into something terrible. "Oliver turned on Zeke. He was feeding information to the sheriff's department. Why would he agree to meet Zeke in a secluded location?"

"He wouldn't," Megan whispered.

"No. He wouldn't." Jax's thoughts raced. "Oliver ran that night. He was terrified, said someone was trying to kill him. You said he had a scuff on his chin, his jacket was missing. There was a fight. Why?" He could see it now, as if watching it unfold in real time. "He arrived at the barn and walked in on a murder. He fought with the killer—then ran, desperate, and called you for help."

"In the car on the night of the accident, Oliver said 'I

shouldn't have trusted him.'" Megan grabbed Jax's arm. "It's someone close to you. To your family. Someone Oliver confided in." Her gaze dropped to the skeleton at their feet. "Someone who killed Zeke in a misguided attempt to protect Oliver. Or help him somehow."

Jax reached into his jacket pocket, wincing as a bolt of pain shot through his injured shoulder. He pulled out the photograph. The one that had been left behind like a taunt. "The killer had this. A picture from Oliver's teenage years. He stole Wesley's identity, opened credit cards in his name, and bought the drone. He framed my brother for the attacks on you."

Megan's eyes widened. "He hates Wesley." Her breath came faster. "He... he hates you. During the first drone attack, he shot at the boathouse. I thought it was to create a distraction, but it wasn't. He was aiming for *you*."

The truth coiled like a viper around his chest as the final missing piece clicked into place.

Jax stilled.

He knew who the killer was.

A creak echoed through the barn.

***

Megan's heart leaped into her throat. She flicked off the flashlight on her phone. Darkness swallowed the room, hiding the skeleton at their feet. But it also deepened the terror clawing through her.

The scrape of a boot against cement was followed by the birds fluttering in the rafters. Someone was definitely in the barn with them. Megan's fingers tightened around the crowbar, her grip so fierce that the metal bit into her palm. She pressed closer to Jax, laying a hand on his back. His muscles were rock solid beneath her touch, his attention focused on the door, gun raised and ready.

"Yoo-hoo. Jax and Megan." The tone was singsong and laced with dark amusement. "I know you're in here. Come out, come out."

She smothered a gasp at the familiar voice. No. It couldn't be.

But it was.

Her colleague. Her friend.

Oliver's friend.

Douglas O'Neal.

A violent shiver wracked her. She'd worked side by side with Douglas since taking the job at Clearview Counseling. They'd shared lunches, swapped case notes, and debated therapy techniques. Just this morning, he'd returned her call about Quinton, assuring her the young man was likely struggling with family issues, but he'd check in on him.

She'd prayed for his mother, who was supposedly in the ICU.

Was she even sick?

Everything Megan thought she knew about Douglas disintegrated. He was a liar. He'd sent her terrifying emails and then worked alongside her, knowing how scared she was. Douglas had attacked her in the woods. He'd tried to kill her with a drone. And yet, he'd smiled and treated her like a friend at the NA meeting. It was beyond duplicitous. It was twisted and sick.

Jax stepped back, forcing Megan with him. Then again. She realized he was guiding her toward the exit door at the rear of the storage room. It meant running back out into the storm, but anything was better than being trapped with a killer.

And Douglas was a killer.

He'd killed Zeke. Oliver. Maybe even others.

Megan's heel knocked against something on the floor. Zeke's bones? Smothering a shudder, she kept her footsteps light as she eased toward the exit. Jax stepped in perfect sync with her, his gun steady, shielding her body with his own.

"Jax, don't be stupid. You and Megan can't escape." Douglas's voice floated through the barn, smooth and confident. "I have a sniper watching the exits. You won't make it into the woods without being shot."

Megan froze. A sinking feeling settled in the pit of her stomach. She rose onto her tiptoes, whispering in Jax's ear. "Quinton."

She didn't know how, but deep down, she knew Douglas had manipulated Quinton into doing his bidding. That was why there were no recent notes in his file. The signs had been there all along. Quinton had confronted her at the coffee shop, pressing her about Oliver's death. Showing up at her office, desperate to talk to Tess, torn apart because someone he trusted had asked him to do something that was *wrong*, but also *right*.

Douglas convinced Quinton that Megan had killed

Oliver and gotten away with it. And for that, she had to die.

Quinton had bought a gun.

Fear tasted bitter in Megan's mouth as the full realization of what they were dealing with crashed over her. There was a murderer in the barn and a potential killer outside.

They were trapped.

Dear God above, what do we do now?

TWENTY-SIX

Escape wasn't possible.

Jax remained motionless, forcing his mind to process the options instead of reacting on instinct. One wrong move could get both him and Megan killed. He had to be strategic. To shut down his emotions. Relying on his training was the only way they'd survive this.

That, and prayer.

Heavenly Father, give me the wisdom I need.

Noah and Dawson were en route. Jax had lost contact with them, but they knew the location and were heading for the barn. It would take time for them to traverse the woods, and they'd have to approach with caution, but they were coming. He just had to buy them time.

His gaze swept the dimly lit storage room, snagging on a ladder in the corner. It led to a small loft space. Jax crossed the room and tested the wood with his weight. It held. He prayed the beams above were just as sturdy.

Lightning flashed, illuminating the barn in a stark white glow. A thunderous boom followed, shaking the entire structure. Rain hammered against the tin roof, a relentless drumbeat. The storm might work in his favor.

"I'm getting impatient." Douglas's voice still carried that unnerving playfulness, but frustration bled into the edges. "Maybe you need some motivation. Allow me to introduce my guest."

A muffled cry echoed through the barn. Desperate. Panicked.

"Please," Cody pleaded. "I don't want to die. Please—"

The sickening crack of a slap cut him off. Then Douglas's singsong voice rang out, colder than before. "Come out, Jax. Don't make me hunt for you. It'll only make things worse."

Jax didn't want to consider how much worse things could get.

Douglas had them trapped. And now he had a hostage.

He wrapped an arm around Megan's waist and pulled her toward the ladder, pressing her back against his chest. Bending low, he whispered in her ear, "Get into the loft. Spread out your weight and be silent. Noah and Dawson will be here, with backup, soon."

Her head turned, her lips a breath from his. It was too dark to see her expression, but he could feel the tension in her body. "What are you going to do?"

There was no time for an argument. "Don't worry about me."

"I can't." Her voice was thick with tears. "We need to stay together—"

"No." His tone was sharp and harsh, but the mere thought of Megan putting herself in harm's way... it crippled him. Jax leaned closer. Megan's perfume filled his senses and her hair brushed softly against his cheek as he put his mouth near her ear. "I love you."

He felt rather than heard her sharp intake of breath. Jax wished he could see her expression. He should have told her earlier—back at the house, when she'd bared her heart to him. But he'd been too tangled up in his family's grief, still convinced that loving her was a betrayal. Of his family. Of Oliver.

He couldn't have been more wrong.

Loving Megan had changed him. He'd been lost—drowning in guilt and anger—and she had pulled him back, showing him a path forward paved with God's grace. Jax saw people's mistakes. Megan saw their potential. She lived by kindness, forgiveness, and understanding.

She was everything Jax hadn't realized he needed.

"I love you," he whispered again. The timing was horrible, but she had to understand what was at stake. "Please, sweetheart. Do this for me. I can't function unless I know you're safe."

Megan hesitated and then nodded. "Don't you dare get yourself killed, Jax Taylor, or I'll never forgive you."

A ghost of a smile curved his lips at the steel in her voice. Then her mouth brushed against his. Sweet. Tender. Full of promises neither of them could be sure would ever become reality. Then, crowbar in hand, Megan scaled the ladder with the silence and precision of a trained operative. The only sound confirming she'd reached the loft was a faint rustling from the birds in the rafters.

Relief swept through him. She was safe—for now.

Jax turned on his heel, flexing his fingers around his gun to adjust his grip. He eased across the storage room, removed the screwdriver from the door, and cracked it open.

Darkness yawned beyond the threshold. Pitch-black and deadly.

Douglas was out there somewhere. Waiting.

Jax let his eyes adjust before stepping out of the storage room, gun leading the way. There was a slim chance he could sneak up on the man and end this now.

A light flickered to his left. Then it vanished.

Flickered again.

This time, Jax caught the sharp outline of Douglas's face before the lighter's flame dipped to a kerosene lamp at his feet. The wick caught, sending an eerie glow flickering across the concrete floor. Jax remained in the shadows, his gun trained on the man who had once been his brother's best friend.

Douglas was ready for a fight.

He wore a bulletproof vest and a helmet. Night vision goggles dangled from a strap around his neck. He'd swapped his thick-rimmed glasses for contacts. The bottoms of his military-style camo pants were soaked from the rain, and a rifle was slung across his back.

In one hand, he held a lighter.

In the other—a handgun.

The barrel was pressed against the temple of a kneeling man.

Cody.

Zeke's brother was soaked, battered, and shaking. A gag muffled his sobs, his chest heaving with every panicked breath. Jax's gut twisted. The hope of sneaking up on Douglas evaporated. He had positioned himself strategically, a corner at his back, cutting off easy access.

Sticking to the shadows, using a support beam as cover, Jax yelled, "Put down your weapons, Douglas. You're under arrest for murder."

Douglas laughed. Cold and sharp. Then his expression darkened. "Where's Megan?"

Jax wasn't going to answer that question. "Why did you do it? Oliver loved you."

"I didn't kill your brother. Megan did." Douglas tilted his head, voice rising as he projected his next words across the barn. "Listen to me—this can go one of two ways. Either you bring Megan out, or I put a bullet in Cody's head." His tone dripped with malice. "You hear that, Megan? You'll be responsible for another man's death. Or you can choose to save his life."

Jax prayed she would stay put. Douglas had no intention of letting any of them leave this barn alive.

The lighter flickered again. Did Douglas plan to burn the barn down? Even in a thunderstorm, the old structure wouldn't last ten minutes. The thought sent ice through

Jax's veins. But if fire was his plan, why hadn't he started it already?

Then it hit him.

This wasn't just about killing Megan. It had never been just about that.

It was about terrorizing her.

Jax clenched his jaw. Where were Noah and Dawson?

Sweat beaded on his forehead. Could he save both Cody and Megan? What if Douglas did set the barn ablaze? If the flames didn't kill them, then the smoke would. Or the sniper waiting outside.

There were too many unknowns. He needed to stall.

Jax sucked in a deep breath, sent a prayer heavenward, and stepped into the main part of the barn. Every step sent a wave of pain through his bullet wound. Blood seeped out of the bandages, trailing down his hand. He ignored it. All of his attention was locked on the killer in front of him.

"I get it, Douglas. You and Oliver were friends. He defended you against the bullies at school and you were loyal to him. You want to avenge his death. But killing Cody and Megan will only make things worse. You shoot him, and then I'll shoot you. It won't end well for any of us." He eased closer, keeping his gun pointed at the criminal. "Put down your weapon. Let's solve this the right way. The way Oliver would have wanted."

Douglas's nostrils flared, his face twisting with sudden anger. "How do you know what Oliver would have wanted?" His voice rose with fury. "You left him!

You betrayed him! He was hooked on drugs and no one cared but me!"

"That's why you killed Zeke. To protect Oliver."

"He was so stupid. I told him to just walk away from Zeke, but Oliver wanted to be the hero." His voice thickened with emotion, but there was no remorse—only rage. "He gave information to the sheriff's department, and Zeke found out somehow. He threatened him. I didn't have a choice."

Jax shifted, angling for a better position. The bulletproof vest Douglas wore left little room for error if he had to take a shot. "You lured Zeke here. Shot him."

"I needed Oliver to understand that I was the only one who loved him." He jabbed at his chest. "We were brothers. Oliver and me. I would do anything for him."

"But when he found out what you did, he was scared. You tussled. Chased him through the woods, gave his car a flat tire so he couldn't escape."

Douglas's eyes widened, wild with barely controlled emotion. "I just wanted him to listen! If he had just given me the chance to explain, then everything would have been fine." His expression darkened, fury tightening his features. "But Megan showed up. She should've stayed out of it."

Douglas had run them off the road to stop Oliver from telling Megan what he knew. And instead of taking responsibility for his actions, he'd spent the last ten years blaming her.

Jax edged closer. "Megan didn't know anything. That's why you didn't kill her right after the accident."

The birds above their heads rustled. Rain beat against the roof.

"She left town in disgrace. I thought it was enough." Douglas sucked in a deep breath and leveled his gaze at Jax. "But when she came back…"

Jax's stomach twisted. He understood. He hated that he did, but he understood.

"It reopened the wound," he said quietly.

"Megan's the one who should've died that day. Instead, she went on with her life. Went to college, made friends, and spent time with her grandparents. She got ten Christmases, ten birthdays, ten YEARS that didn't belong to her. They were Oliver's. He should be here now, not her." His expression contorted with rage. "I'm going to make her pay for what she's done."

"This isn't the way."

"No, it's not your way." His grip on the gun tightened. "Enough talking. I'm going to count to three, and if Megan doesn't come out, I'll put a bullet in Cody's head."

The older man started hyperventilating, struggling against his bonds in a fruitless attempt to save himself. Jax did his best to ignore the horror scene and focused on trying to get a clean shot. The distance was still too great, the chance slim that he'd be able to take Douglas out. His heart hammered against his rib cage.

"One!" Douglas shouted. "Two!"

A shadow shifted behind Douglas. Jax's heart stopped as Megan lifted the crowbar over her head. His feet began moving just as she slammed the metal rod down on Douglas's head.

He roared in pain, stumbling forward.

Jax's world narrowed to the woman he loved and the man trying to kill her. He increased his speed as Megan swung the crowbar again. The metal bounced off the body armor, ineffective. Douglas leveled his gun.

No! Megan!

Jax lunged.

A gunshot shattered the air.

TWENTY-SEVEN

One week later

Jax adjusted the sling supporting his injured arm, wincing as the stitches in his shoulder pulled. He'd stopped taking painkillers after leaving the hospital a few days ago. The doctors had warned him it would take weeks to heal and that physical therapy would follow.

But he was alive. God had seen him through.

Across the living room, his parents sat close on the sofa, hands clasped together. His mom's eyes were red-rimmed but dry. His dad's expression was drawn, grief etched deep in the lines of his face. Wesley, quiet and still, had wedged himself into an armchair, his massive frame too big for the seat. None of this would be easy for them to hear, but they had asked for the details.

Jax began. "Oliver wanted out from underneath Zeke's thumb, and I suppose he thought the best way to achieve that was to shut down the entire operation. He was working as an informant for the sheriff's department, turning over evidence to prove that Bodybuilders—the gym owned by Zeke and Cody—was a front for an illegal fighting ring and drug business."

"He was trying to do the right thing." Wesley's voice was hollow. He met Jax's gaze. "I didn't know. He didn't tell me."

"He didn't confide in any of us. Maybe Oliver was afraid that he wouldn't be successful. There were drugs in his system when he died, but it gives me some measure of comfort to know he was moving in the right direction."

Valentina nodded. "What happened next?"

Jax's gaze flickered to his father. Greg's jaw was clenched tight, but he gave a stiff nod, signaling Jax to continue.

"Somehow, Zeke found out what Oliver was doing and threatened him. Oliver hadn't been confiding in us, but he had been telling Douglas what was going on. Things were getting dangerous, so Douglas lured Zeke to the barn and killed him. I think, in his mind, he was protecting Oliver. But it backfired. Oliver freaked out, and they fought."

A forensic team had discovered his brother's jacket in a corner of the barn. Blood spatter proved Oliver had been present when Douglas shot Zeke. No wonder his brother was so frantic when he called Megan.

"Oliver escaped the barn but, in his panic, must've gotten turned around in the forest trying to find his car. By the time he did, Douglas had already slashed his tire."

Jax could easily imagine his brother's terror. "Oliver called Megan for help and then hid, waiting for her to come. When she arrived, he got in her car, but Douglas caught up to them. He was desperate to stop Oliver from telling Megan about Zeke's murder, so he ran them off the road. He didn't intend to kill Oliver—or so he says—just talk to him."

"But you think he would have killed him?" Wesley asked with the bluntness of a man who'd been to war and back.

Jax hesitated and then nodded. "Oliver wouldn't have kept Zeke's murder to himself. There's no way to know for sure how Douglas would've reacted, but based on his obsession with our brother, I believe he would've seen it as the ultimate betrayal."

Greg frowned. "Then why didn't he kill Megan that night?"

"He thought she died in the accident. When he found out she survived—but didn't know about Zeke—he figured he was in the clear. That Megan left town shortly thereafter also helped. Honestly, it probably saved her life."

Jax hated that Megan had suffered the judgment of townsfolk and the weight of survivor's guilt, but he was glad she'd had the strength to know her limits and seek a new life elsewhere.

"Douglas blamed Megan for Oliver's death," Jax continued. "It was easier to be angry with her than to accept responsibility for his actions. When she moved back to Knoxville, it reignited Douglas's rage. He was obsessing about her, planning to make her suffer, and then I reopened the investigation into the accident."

Jax winced. He'd unknowingly forced Douglas's hand. "Douglas became worried that we'd uncover Zeke's murder during the investigation. So he formed a plan to kill Megan and frame Wesley for it. He broke into her car and attacked her, but when things went sideways, he went to Plan B. And C. And D. Douglas even recruited his patient to help him."

Quinton had been found in the woods by Noah and Dawson. He'd been armed with a rifle and a shotgun, ready to use both should Megan and Jax escape the barn. During his confession, it was clear he'd been manipulated into helping Douglas. It didn't excuse what he did— Quinton made his own choices—but the court would take his circumstances into account during sentencing.

Wesley scraped a hand down his beard. "Why frame me?"

"Because Douglas blamed you—actually, our whole family—for letting Oliver down. He wanted us to suffer."

He'd almost succeeded too. Douglas hadn't caused the cracks in the family's foundation, but his actions had drawn sharp attention to them. From the haunted look in Wesley's eyes, his brother had come to the same conclusion.

"How does Cody fit into all of this?" Greg asked.

"He's guilty of fraud," Jax answered. "Cody and his mom believed Zeke ran off to avoid being arrested on charges of drug trafficking. They sold his vehicle to a chop shop, but the sale was never registered with the state, which is why we believed he still owned the Explorer. Cody signed Zeke's disability checks and cashed them every month. He split the money with his mother. Neither of them ever reported Zeke missing because they didn't want the checks to stop. It seems neither of them knew Zeke was dead."

Jax believed they suspected it, but he had no way to prove it. And, in the end, he wasn't sure it even mattered.

"Douglas heard through the grapevine that Cody had threatened Megan and me," he continued. "He had Quinton monitor Megan's house. When we left in the middle of the night during the storm, he figured Megan was trying to piece together what'd happened during the accident. That's when he put his plan in motion. He kidnapped Cody, drove to the accident site, and set up his ambush. He intended to kill Megan. Then me. Then Cody. After that, he was going to burn the barn to the ground."

Valentina covered her mouth with her hand in shock. "I still... It's horrific to think how..."

"I know, Mamacita." Jax also didn't like to remember those last moments in the barn. There was a second ladder leading down from the loft behind Douglas, which was how Megan got behind him. Her bravery had likely saved them all. But it had also put her at great risk. If Jax hadn't tackled Douglas in time, he would've shot her.

By God's grace, she'd walked away from the incident unharmed.

Jax adjusted his sling again. His arm throbbed. "This morning, Douglas confessed to everything in exchange for a life sentence without the possibility of parole. There won't be a trial. It's over. Chief Garcia will hold a press conference in an hour to share the news." He locked his gaze on his parents and then shifted to his brother before returning to his dad. "Megan will be officially cleared of any wrongdoing. It'll be part of the announcement."

Silence filled the room. No one spoke. No one met his eye.

Nerves twisted in Jax's gut, but he forged ahead. "There's more. It's not my intention to cause you pain, but I need to be honest. I'm in love with Megan."

Valentina gasped. Greg's jaw tensed. Wesley just looked stunned.

Jax was tempted to stop talking, but his heart wouldn't allow it. His family mattered to him. Deeply. But they'd been hiding from each other for far too long.

"She's going to be a part of my life," he continued, his voice firm. "A big part, I think. I know it may take time to get used to the idea, but I hope—and I pray—that one day you'll find it in your hearts to welcome her. What happened the night Oliver died wasn't her fault. She was only trying to help him. She was a good friend, and nearly paid for it with her life."

Tears spilled down Valentina's cheeks. She turned toward Greg, but he was already rising from the couch. His steps were stiff as he moved to the window, hands braced on his hips, shoulders rigid. He stared out for a long time.

"Losing Oliver broke me." Greg turned. "I was drowning in grief and anger. Blaming myself for what happened. Your mother—" He glanced at Valentina, his expression softening. "—tried to get me to attend counseling with our priest, but I refused. And then we had that argument in Chief Garcia's office." His gaze settled on Jax. "Your question haunted me."

Jax swallowed. He knew which one. "Is this what Oliver would have wanted for us?"

Tears shimmered in his dad's eyes. "He was such a loving child. Always happiest when we were all together. And I realized I was dishonoring his memory by letting my anger and my hurt drive a wedge between us." He laid a hand on Wesley's shoulder but kept his gaze locked on Jax. "I'm sorry, boys. I was so lost in my grief that I didn't take the time to think about what either of you was going through. As your father, it's my job to guide you. We should have faced this tragedy together."

Wesley's jaw clenched, his throat working as if he was fighting back tears. Jax felt his own emotions rising, stinging his eyes.

Valentina wiped at her tears and then straightened, her voice firm. "So, from here on out, we act like a family." She pinned her sons and her husband with a stern look. "Sunday—church. Then lunch afterward."

Jax and Wesley nodded in unison. "Yes, ma'am."

A warm smile broke across Valentina's face, chasing away the sadness like sunlight through storm clouds. "Jax, this Sunday, it should just be us. But I'd like for you to bring Megan the following week." She reached for Greg's hands as he rejoined her on the couch. "We have an apology to make. I hope she can find it in her heart to forgive us."

Jax's heart swelled. It was more than he had hoped for. "I'm pretty sure she already has."

The meeting ended with tight embraces and quiet I-love-yous. When Jax stepped outside into the afternoon sunshine, he felt lighter than he had in years. Birds chirped from the branches of the old oak tree. A squirrel darted across the grass.

Wesley followed him onto the driveway, halting beside Jax's rental SUV. He tucked his hands into the pockets of his worn blue jeans. "So you and Megan, huh?"

Jax leaned against the rental. His vehicle was likely totaled, riddled with too many bullet holes to be salvaged, but the insurance company would make the final call later this week. "Yeah." He exhaled, glancing at his brother. "Listen, Wesley, I'm sorry—"

"Don't." Wesley shook his head sharply. "I've been thinking a lot since the meeting in Chief Garcia's office, too. You were right." He hesitated, as if the admission cost him something. "Since I got home, I've been distant. I don't feel... like myself. I don't know if I ever will. But that shouldn't stop me from being part of this family."

Jax's posture softened. "We care about you."

"I know." A ghost of a smile flickered across Wesley's face before he threw a playful punch at Jax's uninjured shoulder. "You realize that once you bring Megan home for Sunday lunch, Mom's gonna start planning your wedding. She can't help herself."

Jax laughed, but his heart thumped a little harder at the thought. A wife. Kids. It had always felt far off in the distance. But now... he could almost see it. Still, he didn't need his mother dropping hints every five minutes. "Let's not jump the gun. We still have to get through the first Sunday lunch."

Wesley shrugged. "It'll be fine. Later, bro." He started toward his truck, but Jax called after him. Wesley turned back. "Yeah?"

"There's an informal veterans' support group that meets regularly. I think you know some of the guys—Jason Gonzalez?"

"Yeah, I know him."

"It might be good to go. Talking with people who've been through the same things you have could help."

Wesley stared off into the distance for a long moment. "I'll think about it."

It wasn't a yes, but it also wasn't a no. Jax would take it.

He lifted a hand in farewell as Wesley climbed into his truck, then slid into his own vehicle. For the first time in years, he felt something close to peace.

Then, finally, he let the excitement settle in—the realization of what he truly wanted. He was in love. He wanted a future with Megan. And after this conversation with his family, for the first time, it seemed possible.

It was time to set things right with the woman of his dreams.

TWENTY-EIGHT

A breeze rippled across the lake, sending gentle waves lapping against the dock and lifting strands of Megan's hair. Ducks swam lazily past, gliding over the water's shimmering surface. Sunshine warmed her shoulders. Across the yard, her grandparents' voices drifted in easy conversation as they debated where to plant the tomatoes for their garden. She smiled at the sound of Nana's laugh.

They were happy. The threats were over, the criminals locked up. All was right in the world.

Almost, anyway.

As she had so many times in the past week, Megan thought of Jax. They'd spoken a few times. She'd visited him in the hospital. But neither of them had brought up their future. She understood, without him telling her, that he needed space. Love didn't fix everything. Their history was complicated, tangled up in grief and old wounds. And even if—and it was a big if—they pursued a relationship, it would affect Jax's family.

They might never accept her.

Megan had made peace with that. If Jax walked away, she would be gracious. It would shatter her heart, but she would never come between him and the people he loved. The Taylors had endured enough loss.

The scrape of a boot against the dock cut through her thoughts. A long shadow fell over her, momentarily blocking out the sun. Megan's heart skipped a beat. Any bravery she'd been building crumbled the second she met Jax's gaze.

"Hey." His lips curved into a devastating smile. "Mind if I join you?"

She nodded, not trusting herself to speak.

Jax lowered himself beside her, his long legs dangling over the edge. His nearness sent a riot of butterflies fluttering through her stomach. She tried to push them down, but it was impossible. He had an effect on her that couldn't be wrangled.

Her gaze dropped to the sling cradling his arm. "How's your shoulder?"

"It still hurts, but it's healing." He drew in a deep breath and nodded toward the scorched patch in her yard. "I see you hauled away the boathouse."

"Pops took care of it." Megan glanced behind her and nearly groaned. Her grandparents were not-so-subtly watching them from the porch. She scowled and waved behind Jax's back, signaling them to stop staring. So embarrassing.

Jax chuckled, missing nothing. "Your grandparents

are happy." His lips quirked. "I dare say, I think your grandfather might like me now."

Megan laughed. "You've come a long way with Pops, that's true. I think it was the press conference that finally won him over. Chief Garcia announced I was officially cleared of any wrongdoing." She nudged Jax lightly with her shoulder. "Thank you."

"For what? Chief Garcia told the truth, that's all."

She arched a brow. "Dawson already ratted you out. He let it slip that you specifically asked the chief to include that in the announcement."

Jax didn't respond, just gave her a quiet, almost bashful look. Megan's heart squeezed. Even now, even after everything, he was still protecting her.

"It means a lot," she murmured.

His gaze lingered on her face before flickering out toward the lake. Tension rolled off him, subtle but unmistakable. Megan tensed in response.

"What is it?"

"I spoke to my family this afternoon."

"Oh." She winced, bracing herself for heartbreak.

"I told them I'm in love with you." Megan's breath stalled. Jax said it so casually, like it was something he'd been saying to her for years. Like it was the most natural thing in the world. "And that I want you to be a part of my life. A big part."

She stared, unsure if she'd heard him right.

"They'd like you to come to Sunday lunch," he continued. "In two weeks. So... I guess I'm asking if you'd like to."

Megan blinked. "Your family wants me to come to Sunday lunch?" Her voice was laced with disbelief. "But what about—"

"It was never your fault. And finally, my family is ready to heal." His gaze searched hers, questioning. Then he swallowed hard. "But if your feelings have changed, that's okay. Just say so. It was a crazy week, with a maniac trying to kill us, and—well, we can continue on as friends."

She sucked in a breath, her pulse hammering. "No, Jax. We can never be friends."

His face fell, just slightly, but before he could react, Megan reached up and cupped his cheek. "I could never be just your friend," she whispered. "I love you too much for that."

Relief crashed through his expression. "Oh, thank God. I was worried for a second that I was going to have to be your friend while being hopelessly in love with you." His lips tilted. "Pretty sure that would be harder than being your enemy."

"You were never my enemy. I didn't like you much, but you weren't my enemy."

Jax threw his head back and laughed, the rich sound carrying on the wind, filling Megan's chest with warmth. She could spend forever like this—sitting on a dock, next to Jax, listening to him laugh.

Then he looked at her, and all the air fled her lungs.

Megan's heart tumbled over itself as he leaned in, his lips brushing against hers in a whisper-soft touch. The world faded, shrinking to nothing but him—this moment, this man. Jax kissed her like he had all the time in the world, like he was memorizing her. His good arm wrapped around her, pulling her close, anchoring her against him. The heat of his palm pressed into her lower back, sending shivers up her spine.

Megan melted into him, her hands sliding up his chest, feeling the steady thrum of his heartbeat beneath her fingertips.

No, she took it back.

She could spend the rest of her life like this.

Sitting on a dock.

Kissing the man she loved.

Dawson hit save on his report and scrubbed a hand over his tired eyes. It had been one exhausting day. He reached for the coffee mug sitting on a warmer and scowled at the empty bottom. Maybe it was for the best. He'd had enough caffeine to fuel a jet.

But they'd put a murderer away for life. Not too shabby.

"What are you still doing here?" Noah poked his head over the top of Dawson's cubicle. "Weren't you supposed to go home an hour ago?"

The chief had ordered him to clock out, but Dawson hated leaving without filing his reports. "Just finishing up." His gaze swept over his fellow detective. Noah looked worse for wear after working around the clock for the last week. His hair stood up in spikes, and the bags under his eyes were deep enough to look permanent. "You aren't on duty tomorrow, are you?"

Noah shook his head. "I'm spending the day with my wife." He grimaced. "Provided she remembers we're still married. I haven't seen Felicity in days. Every time I popped home to check on Harper, she was gone. She's been working a big case too."

Noah's wife was a Texas Ranger.

Dawson grinned. "Going through withdrawal?"

"Yep, and not ashamed to admit it." Noah grinned. "There's only two things in life I need. My daughter and my wife. Not necessarily in that order, mind you, but it's hard when work takes me away from them."

A pang ricocheted through Dawson's chest. There had been a time he'd felt the same way—when going home at the end of a long shift meant seeing the woman he loved. But those days were long over. Tragedy had shattered his marriage. And his heart.

Noah tapped on the top of the cubicle, pulling Dawson from his thoughts. "Go home, man. You look ready to drop."

"I will." He had one more report to get through first. "Good work, by the way."

"You too." Noah fist-bumped him. "We make a good team."

"Yes we do."

They'd come perilously close to losing Megan and Jax. If they'd arrived at the barn even a minute later... Dawson didn't let himself finish the thought.

"Night, Noah. Give my love to Felicity and Harper."

Noah yawned and nodded, waving as he headed for the front door.

Silence settled over the station. Dawson liked it when things were quiet. It was so different from the constant chaos of the Dallas Police Department, where he'd worked for ten years before coming home to Knoxville. Scrubbing his hands down his face, he opened his eyes wide and set his jaw. "Okay. Last report, then I'm out."

He clicked on the document and started typing. Just as he was about to finish, his cell phone rang.

He answered it absently. "This is Graham."

"Dawson."

He froze as the all-too-familiar voice spilled from the Bluetooth speaker in his ear.

Peyton.

His ex-wife.

"I'm sure... I know this isn't..." She muttered something under her breath and then inhaled sharply. "I need your help, Dawson. It's a matter of life and death."

Texas Ranger Heroes Series

Ranger Protection

Ranger Redemption

Ranger Courage

Ranger Faith

Ranger Honor

Ranger Justice

Ranger Integrity

Ranger Loyalty

Ranger Bravery

Ranger Purpose

Triumph Over Adversity Series

Calculated Risk

Critical Error

Necessary Peril

Strategic Plan

Covert Mission

Tactical Force

Badge of Honor Series

Fractured Memories

Dangerous Lies

Would you like to know when my next book is released? Or when my novels go on sale? It's easy. Subscribe to my newsletter at www.lynnshannon.com and all of the info will come straight to your inbox!

Reviews help readers find books. Please consider leaving a review at your favorite place of purchase or anywhere you discover new books. Thank you.

www.ingramcontent.com/pod-product-compliance
Lightning Source LLC
Chambersburg PA
CBHW061810190726

48289CB00007B/2139